D1242294

SAM'S LADY

MURIEL S. WRIGHT

LUCKY BOOKS
Winchester, VA.

Published by
Lucky Books
P.O. Box 1415
Winchester, VA 22601

ISBN: 0-922510-09-1

Printed in the United States of America

March 1994

10 9 8 7 6 5 4 3 2 1

M&G

My thanks to my dedicated husband—Chas, not to mention being loving and patient.

I love thee, I love but thee,
With a love that shall not die
Till the sun grows cold,
And the stars are old,
And the leaves of the Judgment Book
unfold!

Bayard Taylor—Bedouin Song

INTRODUCTION

This is a love story, tried and true. There is no plot, no suspense, and no murder.

However, the author believes that by the time you read the last page, you will have fallen in love with these two people.

Penny writes for a newspaper and Sam is a war correspondent. They knew each other at the University of Virginia, and now they've met again, after many years, in Washington D.C. The year is 1954.

CHAPTER I

1954

"SAM! MY God—Sam Boyer!

He stood there leaning against the door frame just as nonchalant as though they had seen each other a week earlier. (Geez it didn't matter when she'd see this guy, he made her legs go weak) There were times when she wished he'd get out of her life and stay out, and at other times like right now, when he made her so happy just to see him again.

"Well, does an old friend get invited in or does he stand here in the hall." (She was still more woman than any he'd ever met and he'd about decided that he'd never really know, for sure). After a bear hug initiated by Sam, he began inviting himself in. She was apologizing for her appearance.

"It was thoughtful of you to let me know you were coming so I could primp up, you devil. Just look at me in old pants, baggy shirt, and a pony tail that

1

looks more like a mane. (Her eyes covered her appearance in one quick distasteful glance.) My mom told me there would be days like this, and she was right. Oh, well now you've seen the real me."

"Believe me, there's nothing wrong with the real you." (He was looking her over, too).

"You must have just gotten back from one of those foreign assignments when just about any American girl looks good. You were in Korea, right? No excuses Sam, sit down, I take compliments from anyone, anytime."

He got out a cigarette, lit up, and placed the burned match on the smoke stand. His eyes remained glued on her as she sat across from him on the sofa. She never changed! They'd seen each other maybe five or six times since college days in the late thirties, and she still had that same willowy figure and boobs that a big shirt couldn't hide. Damn it!

Why didn't she get a bulge some place or a double chin. Oh no, if anything she improved with age. Penny wasn't beautiful, not really, but God the aura of sex appeal surrounding her became greater and even more pronounced as she grew older. How does that happen, he wondered. That's not the way nature is supposed to work. His eyes settled on her faltering pony tail of "dirty blond" hair (as she always referred to it) and somehow it looked just right. She had just asked him something, and he didn't even hear the question—he was lost in his own thoughts. She used to tell him that she had eyes like her papa even though his were brown. But then no one could have eyes like Penny. They were so darn blue that even her eyelids reflected the color. Her eyes were peaceful and yet very much alive. He wondered what her papa looked like. Just then she snapped her fingers at him.

"Remember me, Penny Nagel. I just asked how you found me?"

He knocked the ash from his cigarette, and apologized for daydreaming, and told her that he'd been by the Post. When he found out she was on the staff —getting her address was a piece of cake.

"I guess they told you that I'm leaving. Next week I'm out of here."

He looked surprised. "No, I guess the kid that I talked to didn't know. As he flattened the cigarette butt in the ashtray, he looked at her once again, and said, "Well, my timing was just right then, wouldn't you say. Where are you off to?" (Then he noticed a few boxes in the hall)

"Oh Sam, this big newspaper deal isn't for me. You know I'm a small town girl and I just never did feel as though I fit in—so I've been working on other options. I suppose I'm in awe of the big city and the big city newspaper. Actually, I realized this some time ago, but you think twice before resigning a position of this magnitude." She laughed and shook her head, "I don't want to bore you with my aspirations. What about you? Your life is the one with the war experiences, adventure, and excitement," she said with great flourish.

"Pen you haven't changed. You always had the mistaken idea that my career was so great and terrific as compared to yours, and that's just not true. Fulfillment is the key and my key is just shaped differently. It's not better nor is it more rewarding, it's just

different. Oh well, that's a moot point and I didn't
come to see you for that reason. Do you have plans
for tonight?"

Penny didn't. She wished she had. Tomorrow
night she did. Oh damn, why lie. She and Sam were
old friends. If he wanted to think she never had
dates, who cares. "No—just packing boxes. I'm on
vacation until I leave here."

His face lit up. "Good, let's go out for dinner and
we can reminisce. We've got almost five years to
cover this time." (He remembered. Did she?)

"Are you here to stay?"

"Only if you extend the invitation."

"Oh Sam, come on, you know what I mean. Tell
me about Connie and your son."

"I told you we had a lot of years to cover. You
know I'm divorced and Connie went back to Illinois.
She never really liked any place that we lived—not
like *her* home anyway."

He stood up then, and walked over to the window
which looked out on the front yard. He said, as he
turned to face her, "I expected my wife to enjoy
living with me when we were married, but I guess it
doesn't always work that way. My son, Cal, well you
know the courts, the child always goes to Mama,
especially when they're young. God Pen, I tried, especially for the boy's sake, but it just didn't work out.
We never had a divorce in our family and it just
about killed my parents." He jammed his hands in
his pockets, and as he looked away from her there
was a huskiness in his voice, "That kid is so damned
good. He even looks like me."

"Oh Sam, I am so sorry. You do get to see him surely."

"Oh sure on Thanksgiving, never Christmas, and then big times in the summer. Hell, that's no way to raise a kid. You know what kind of a schedule a journalist has. Many times when it suits me, he's in school and of course, there are times in the summer when it really doesn't suit me." He had come back to the chair and pulled out another cigarette. "Excuse the expression Pen, but sometimes life's a bitch. Well, we covered some ground there." As he dragged on his cigarette, he asked, "What about you—no one special in your life?"

"Not *that* special." She pulled off her sneakers and tucked her feet under her. Geez, she thought, why didn't she throw those sneaks away. They really looked awful.

Laughing, he shook his head from side to side, but he was eye balling her shoes.

"There's a joke?" She was tickled.

"Why don't you throw those darn shoes away. Penny they've had it. (Lord, she was frugal as ever.) You haven't changed a bit. Do you still have that sign you flashed around at school. I think it was one of Ben Franklin's gems regarding 'a penny saved'." Sam remembered that Penny's stepfather had taken his own life during the depression when he went broke.

"Sure, I just packed it yesterday. Geez Sam, you never learned a thing having lived through the depression, did you."

He just sat back amused. She was great when she

was on her soap box regarding the importance of saving.

Then he decided to surprise her. "Oh I remember, 'A penny saved is two pence clear, A pin a day's a groat a year'. HA, you thought I forgot." He laughed, pointing a finger at her.

"All right you win, and I will have dinner with you tonight; however, it'll cost many times more than a groat."

"The cost I can manage. I just hope you didn't pack all your shoes." After that remark, they burst into laughter again. (What the hell was the value of a groat.) Oh well, he decided, it wasn't important anyway.

"Before we got sidetracked discussing a certain item of my attire, I had asked you if you were in Washington to stay?"

"I'm not sure. Sometimes I think I'd like to get into television. Reporting news through a different medium might be a pleasant change. However, I'm getting older by the minute—so I need to forge ahead now if I want to give it a shot."

Penny started to laugh again, since she didn't even notice any gray hairs nor a receding hairline. He still looked trim and fit and so darn handsome it was frightening. She knew he had to be past 35, and who would guess it. Her boss at the Post was 42 and he looked so much older. (I wonder if he dyes his hair.)

"What's so funny this time? You know how old I am, I can't fool you."

"Okay. Truth now. Since I know how old you are, do you dye your hair."

"Do I what?" he asked, raising an eyebrow in disbelief. "Do I dye my hair?" He repeated. Then he laughed, and said, "Of course, didn't you know I'm really a red head."

She casually walked over to where he sat, and began examining his slicked down George Raft hairstyle with her fingers. "Whoops, wrong again, I found a few gray ones. Do you want me to take care of them?" (She pulled out a gray hair with a quick jerk of her fingers.)

"Ouch! I'll take care of you." He caught her wrist and pulled her gently onto his lap. And then, his lips found hers as they had on other visits. He kissed her tenderly at first, and then with an unbridled passion.

Her kissing with Sam, except for one visit back in the late forties when he was happily married, always left her wanting more. He pulled her hard against his chest and her arms went around his neck, and they just couldn't let go for a long period of time.

Finally when they came up for air, although they were still just inches apart, Sam said very softly, as his fingers wound through her now loose hair, "Oh Penny we fit so well together."

He still had that same woodsy smell that he had back in college and of all the shaving lotions she'd smelled during all these years—only Sam's really got to her. She slowly rubbed her finger over just the beginning of a "five o'clock shadow," and smiling said, "I know, and I've missed your special touch."

His eyes were smiling into hers now, as he said, rather amused, "Even better than that guy Brady you told me about last time we were together."

She threw her head back, and looked him straight in the eyes, "Good gosh that had to be at least four years ago. Brady turned out to be a dud. I've had better since then, but they're all after my money." (She laughed)

"I'm not." He was serious again.

"Oh, I know you're not. I already know what you're after."

He pulled her to him for another round of passionate kissing and she could feel a hardness in his lap. She could also feel the hot sensations pulsating throughout her body that only Sam could arouse in her. Oh God, she thought, move out of his lap—NOW!

She felt drained as she reluctantly pulled away. "If this is the appetizer, I'm already in fear of the dessert." She trembled.

He put his arms around her waist, "So what else is new. You've always been in fear of the dessert, that's why I've never tasted it."

Lord, here we go again. He knew how she felt about premarital sex. That's why she was still a virgin at 33, and not ashamed of it. She knew it was very likely that she would go to her grave without ever having experienced the joy and love her parents shared in the act, but call her square, she felt that final step of love-making should be reserved for her husband. Her papa, Reverend Nagel, and her mother, Rebecca Nagel, taught her morals growing up that she felt compelled to live by. Sam had always been very special to her, but Lord he sure tried her patience.

"Let's not argue." She stood up and walked toward her kitchen. "Could I get you a drink?"

"That's a poor substitute for what I'd really like,

but if you've got a beer—I'll take it." (This Sam she could handle.)

"You've got a nasty mouth Boyer. Just for that you can drink out of the bottle." She flipped off the cap, and as the fizz shot up in his face, he said, "I owe you one," and snapped her on the rump. As she picked up her sneakers, she threw him a paper towel and headed down the hall. Moving away, she called, "I'll get on my glad rags—won't take me long." (She was still against the masses, he thought, wiping off his face)

He waited as long as he could, and after he heard the shower go off, he called down the hall, "Is there another bathroom?"

The bathroom door came open a crack, "Did you call?"

"Yes, I asked if there is another bathroom?"

"Why?" Her voice rang out loud and clear.

"I wanted to study the fixtures and color scheme and I need to right now."

When he started down the hall, she flew out of the bathroom wrapped in a huge towel. All he could see was her calves and ankles, and her shoulders, and he'd seen all those before. Damn!

Beer just seemed to have a way of going right through him—non-stop. After he washed his hands and looked in the mirror, he detected the beginning of unwanted whiskers. Damn beard. He opened the door and called out to Pen, who was singing in her bedroom, "Do you have a razor I could use?" My God what was she singing. He couldn't recognize the tune and certainly not the words. He called again—louder. This time her door came open a crack. He started yelling again then brought his voice down a notch since all was quiet now. "Do you have a razor I could use?"

"Why?"

"I want to shave my legs."

"Oh sure, it's in that drawer to the far left—way in the back. I don't want anyone to know that I shave."

"Why?" (Two can play this game, he thought)

"My beard, what else," she laughed, closed her door and began singing again.

He stood there a second or two, shook his head, and left her pleasant bathroom aroma sink into his nostrils. Nothing smelled better than a bathroom right after a woman finished bathing. He missed that, now that he was alone again. As he turned toward the drawer, he noticed her jeans, shirt, and undies on a pile in the corner. She'd be mortified if he mentioned it. She was so crazy-clean—always. She had left in a hurry when she heard him coming down the hall. When he pulled out the drawer, there were her toilet articles. He smelled the same tangy body lotion that she must have used. There was a skin cream, arrid deodorant, and a few tampons. Then, just as she said, way in the back was the razor. He guessed it was too much to expect some shaving cream. Yeah, too much to expect. So he scraped the blade rather grudgingly over his tough bristles, ran his hand over the rough spots and decided it would have to do for now. He couldn't even find any extra blades. She'd probably used that one for her legs all year. Oh, well it would serve her right if their love making caused her cheeks to get scratched. In fact, he decided that wasn't a bad idea. The singing had

stopped and she bounced through the open bathroom door wiggling into a sexy, little black dress. She
turned her back to him.

"Sam, please a little help with the zipper."

With her back stuck in his face and her zipper
going up from the waist, his task began. He was
tempted to say it caught on her bra which was also
black and very visible, but instead remarked, "You
must really be poured into this baby (making his
progress deliberately slow). I'm dying to see it from
the front."

"Sam for now concentrate on the zipper, please.
Later I'll turn around." She sounded very impatient.

"Steady she goes—let's mind our temper Penny.
What would you do if I wasn't here to help you
dress?"

As she turned around he could smell that tangy
aroma again, but her comment changed the moment. "If you weren't here, I'd still be in my jeans."
Just then she noticed her pile of dirty clothes. She
hurried over and scooped them up—dropping the
panties twice before she secured all items of clothing
and rushed from the bathroom.

He laughed and laughed, and called after her as
she rushed into her bedroom, "I still haven't seen
the dress from the front."

They met head-on in the hall. She made a a curtsy
and turned completely around once. "Do I meet
with your approval?"

"Oh-h yes." Penny had that Doris Day kind of
wholesomeness. The black dress was fitted to the
waist, and then the skirt flared out. She wore very
little make-up, and her hair wasn't quite dry, but

geez she looked so good. She was just so refreshing and virginal (which he believed she still was). He remembered on one of his visits when they got into a deep discussion on sex before marriage which he knew she was opposed to when he told her that 'she thrashed around in the throes of eternal darkness knowing there could be no end'—that really set her off. She really laid into him. He'd never forget her remarks. "Just because you're a world-renown correspondent and journalist, and presumably a Don Juan on every continent doesn't give you the right to lecture me with these crazy quotes that aren't worth a pile of shit." That was the first and last time he'd heard her use that word. He limited his comments now to one-liners that were his own and not a quote he'd absorbed from some think tank.

"Maybe I should have gone back to my motel and changed or suggested that you remain in your jeans. Where does one take such a gorgeous dish in Alexandria?"

Sam looked like Sam—didn't matter how he dressed. He looked good in jeans, baggy pants, suit, or a tux. He never looked perfectly groomed and never would. That just wasn't Sam. Right now his tie was a little wilted, his coat should have been pressed, and his shoes didn't shine, but when was a journalist ever well-groomed. Now his hair, although straight, was most always combed and slicked down. She'd never seen it any other way.

"Flattery will get you somewhere—now let's just see where." As she picked up the phone book, she said, "Oh yes, if I remember correctly, rare steak was a big favorite.

"Then again seafood ranked quite high on your list also. I know a good restaurant for which ever you prefer." Her finger moved down the page, as she suggested that reservations might be in order. "For Pete's sake," she said, glancing up, "stop looking at me like that—you have seen me in a dress before."

He had struck a pose with his forefinger resting against his lips and studying her legs intently, he said, "Your seams are crooked."

"Oh geez," and she stretched her head around to view the back of her sheer, black hose which covered a perfect set of legs and ankles. "Sam you devil, they're all right."

"Yes, you could say that. However, I think they're better than all right. Are you sure those seams don't need to be straightened? Steak's fine," he added, still giving her legs close scrutiny.

"You're impossible." Her cheeks were flushed and she realized that she felt much safer when he was happily married and almost said as much, but decided that remark would be in poor taste.

As she hunted the number, he came over and put his arms around her waist, "I didn't mean to embarrass a fellow journalist—sorry love." (He kissed her on the neck and stepped back.)

She was clearly flustered as she replaced the phone in the cradle. It was so hard for her to concentrate on restaurant listings and whether or not reservations were necessary when he talked about feeling her legs and kissing her on the neck, but she tried her best to appear in control, as she said, "If we leave right now, we don't need reservations. Okay, Lover Boy."

He stepped back, put both arms up, palms out,

and said, "Sorry, I'll behave." He put her coat
around her shoulders, and they left the apartment.

She thought again of their conversation regarding
his failed marriage. She had deliberately changed the
subject at the time 'cause she realized his mood was
about to hit rock bottom. God, he really loved that
little boy. The look that came into his eyes when he
talked of his visits. There was a time years ago when
Penny didn't believe that Sam Boyer really knew how
to love. But today she found out that he definitely
knew how to love a son. She truly believed that Sam
had the power to generate sex from any woman with
whom he chose. He had that much charisma and sex
appeal. She knew without his mentioning, that he
had to marry Connie since Cal was born six months
later. Had he loved her? He had never gone into
great detail with her about that part of his life, but
she also knew he would. She was probably the only
woman he regarded as a friend rather than a sex part-
ner. (She'd laid the ground rules a long time ago)
There were no regrets. She just wished with all her
heart and soul that somewhere out there she would
find a man who truly wanted Penny Nagel, and not
because she was a good "lay." Sam had all the attri-
butes she'd ever wanted, unfortunately he wasn't in
love with her. She knew he wanted her but not for
the right reasons. She glanced over at his profile in
the semi-darkness and wondered what he was thinking.

"Okay Penny, do I go straight here or turn right."
(So much for what he was thinking)

"Have I ever let you down?"

"No, damn it."

"Boyer that mouth is going to get you into trouble. Oh darn, you should have turned right."

"I knew it. Every time I even hint at sex you get frustrated."

"If we miss that meal 'cause we don't have reservations, you're going to be frustrated, not to mention hungry."

"This should be Ashlawn—turn right here. Okay now turn right again and we'll be on the route."

"Thanks, but I could have figured that out. Now what's the name again. Oh, I remember, Blackbeard."

"No, it's the Black Steer."

"Well, I was close. After all, I was kissing your neck when you spouted out the name."

"That's it down there on the right. If you turn in here, there's parking in the back." (she pointed)

"When did you start on white wine?" They were studying the menu after being seated in a secluded corner with the glow of the candle playing havoc with her eyes and unadorned neck.

"Oh I don't know, but it must have been since I saw you last if you don't remember." Her fingers curled around the stem and she took another sip.

"Pen this is very romantic and I do appreciate your taste in this sexy setting, but I wonder if I'll be able to see my steak or even know if it's rare."

"That's gratitude. I paid extra for this location. We could have been seated closer to the bar, but knowing you I was sure you'd prefer dining by candlelight."

"Not complaining—surprised, maybe. I didn't know that I had that effect on you."

"If you must know, there was another reason—you won't notice me blush quite as easily." (She'd been doing a lot of that lately)

"That's not true and you know it. You just want to see me wear my glasses."

She looked surprised.

"I told you that I needed to forge ahead."

Just then the waiter appeared for their order and Sam reached for his inside pocket and came out with his glasses.

Penny suppressed her chuckle, and thought how dignified he looked—even rather sophisticated.

Once they had placed their order, the waiter left with the menus, and Sam had removed his glasses, he said, "Now why do you think that I'm going to make you blush?" He filled their wine glasses.

"You look so cute. I love your choice of frames—they add dignity."

"I think I'll feel your leg." His right arm quickly disappeared beneath the white tablecloth. His hand touched her knee.

She moved back slightly, as she said, "Sam Boyer don't you dare." (He didn't call that blushing)

He laughed as he brought his hand back to the table. "Dignity," he growled, "and you write for the Post."

"Did write for the Post."

"You never did tell me. Where is your next job?"

"Small newspaper—small town, and I've written a book. Don't laugh. I know that I'll never gain anywhere near your status, but it's something that I always wanted to do—just for my own enjoyment."

"That's not fair. I'd never laugh at you—you're

too good in your field. Where? You haven't told me yet."

"Well, it's Lancaster, Pennsylvania. You know my parents live in the suburbs of Philadelphia, and Lancaster is about 60 miles west. I sent out approximately nine letters of application, and working on the Lancaster New Era, a daily afternoon paper, seemed to be the right deal. You know I was born and raised close to there."

There was an excitement in her voice which he couldn't miss, and he was sure that newspaper felt lucky to land her. He took another drag from his cigarette before asking her when she would begin.

"April 1. I have some misgivings concerning my first day being April Fool's Day, but that's what my contract says. What do you think?"

He covered her hand with his as it lay on the table. "That doesn't mean a damn thing—that Lancaster New Era can thank their lucky stars that Penny Nagel's coming to work for them." (He was serious. She knew his moods and almost felt like crying.)

"Oh Sam, you really think so?" He picked up her hand and kissed it, "I know so."

She had a way of getting under his skin and right now was one of those times. God, she was so sincere and naive—there was no way she could be in her thirties, but he knew differently. He knew Lancaster to be a farming community and it wouldn't be long until one of those farmers had Penny at the altar. Somehow he didn't want to think about her being married. Before he could ask her about her book, the waiter arrived with their order.

They wasted little time in diving into their delicious looking steaks. Once again Sam put on his glasses. He really did want to see if it was done to his satisfaction. The waiter waited politely until Sam gave his seal of approval.

"Sam whether you believe it or not, I did eat lunch today, but these rolls are just delicious."

"You're the only woman I know who can eat as much as I do and still not gain weight. What was your lunch?"

"Is this information really important? I mean, you know, are we going to compare weights?"

"That's a thought. However, I was just curious to know what the average working girl eats for lunch."

"Very little. Of course, right now I'm not working and I begin my lunch when I awake in the morning and continue on through until about 1 p.m.

"Oh then you eat this yogurt I've been hearing so much about."

"Lord, no. I hate it. I'm a soup and sandwich girl. How's your steak?"

"Perfecto." He touched his thumb to his index finger and held up his hand to make his point. "Just the way I like it."

"Good. I knew this was an excellent restaurant that's why I selected it."

"Do you come here often?" he asked, as he doused his baked potato with sour cream.

"Depends on what you mean by *often?*"

"Once a week with the guy that's not *that* special."

"No. We hit the Italian restaurant or Chinese, usually."

"Is he with the government?"

"He's with NACA."

"What does he think about your leaving the area?"

"That I don't like it enough to stay here." (She had just finished off her *not* so rare steak.)

"You're a journalist all right—no doubt about that."

CHAPTER II

HE WIPED his mouth with his napkin, and then looked at her with mischief in his eyes, as he said, "How about dessert?"

She met his look straight on, "Depends on what it is."

"Oh God, Pen you know what it is, but you still haven't joined the masses." He finished off his beer. "No dessert, am I right?" She nodded. He was serious again and she was too.

She laughed nervously, and he picked up on it.

"Will I be the first to know when you drop your guard?"

"No, my husband will be the first, but I do have some cookies at home that I baked this morning."

"Are you inviting me to your apartment, friend?"

"Of course, we haven't scratched the surface yet on all the news we need to catch up on."

They were quiet on the return trip, and each was doing a lot of thinking.

She remembered the first time she met him at U. Va. She was a freshman and he was a junior and he was already involved in newspaper work. The following year he was editor. No one knew, not even her parents, it was due to Sam's influence that she changed her major to journalism. She actually had wanted to be a doctor like her Aunt Mim. He had such a profound effect on her. Even as an underclassman and playing a very minor role on the newspaper staff, he had always made her feel very special, when she knew very well she wasn't. She also knew his reputation as a ladies man but regardless of all the gossip, he never once stepped out of line with her. He always included her in every aspect of college life and actually made her college days ones to look back on with fond memories. She would never forget the first time he kissed her. He was leaving right after graduation and going overseas as a military journalist. Ernie Pyle was his idol. The newspaper staff had a party for him and all the girls lined up to kiss him good-bye. Pen stayed in the background. She just couldn't appear to take his kiss so lightly. He sought her out, and they kissed good-bye with no one around. That was her first experience with an erotic kiss. Her high school boyfriends didn't do that. At first, she was repulsed by it, but then as they did it over and over again, she felt a delirious sensual feeling and sexual arousal that she would never forget. She didn't! All he said was that he had wanted to kiss her from the first time he had seen her. Their eyes met and held and his last words were "I'll keep in touch." She missed him at graduation and never saw him again before he left for overseas. But he wrote to her at college and through the years, they never lost contact. He had kept his word and he was her oldest friend.

"Damn, would you believe I'm lost." He slowed down and peered out as he wound down the window. It had started to rain and visibility wasn't all that great. "What do you say co-pilot?"

"I say you're right again, we're lost. Actually, I think we're in the District. Have you been to the Lincoln Memorial lately?"

"No, but I believe we're going to make Abe a visit." It wasn't too long until she spouted out new directions.

"Turn right here and circle around."

"Aye, aye cap-i-tan." He saluted Penny and swung the car around into a parking space.

It was rather late for tourists; consequently there were few people in the area when Sam got out and walked around to Penny's side of the car. As he opened her door, he bent over and graciously invited her to visit with the 16th president of the United States. The rain had almost completely stopped, but the grass was wet.

Sam took her hand and she carried her shoes in the other. As they stood there in silence and looked up at the famous statue, they were awed by the profound significance of this great president. "This is what I'll miss most when leaving here. All I have to do is visit the many memorials, and I'm reminded again of what a great country we live in and how fortunate I am to be an American. My papa is very patriotic. He was a soldier in World War I and fought in France."

Sam was quiet. He'd seen war at its worst, and he knew also what a great feeling it was to once again plant his feet on American soil.

"You're thinking about the war, too, aren't you, or maybe the one we've just gotten ourselves out of. God, wouldn't it be great if there weren't any more wars."

Her voice was filled with so much compassion, as he looked at her standing in her stocking feet and tears in her eyes. He put his arm around her shoulders, "Oh, Pen, war is horrible. There aren't any good wars, and I'm sure your papa would agree. Necessary, maybe, but not good." (Like that terrible medicine his mother made him take when he had a cold. She'd keep saying this is good for you. Sam would say not good, but necessary.)

Oh yes, Penny knew about war. Harrison and Lawrence, her twin brothers, had experienced the horrors. Only Harrison had been in the thick of it, but they had both served in Korea. Thank God, David was spared. He was ready to go, when President Eisenhower negotiated a truce last year.

They stood there in silence for awhile longer just thinking about war being bitter medicine. Feeling they were so insignificant and yet in a way, important, too.

Hand-in-hand they walked slowly back to the car. Once they were settled in the front seat, Pen looked at Sam, and said, "Well, between the two of us I hope we can find our way back to my apartment." (She yawned.)

"If you fall asleep and I need directions, I'll call you." It wasn't long until her head fell onto his shoulder and he decided to test left-handed driving. After he turned off the motor, once he had pulled into the space alongside her car, he sat there for a few seconds. All quiet except for some speeder on the next block. He bent over and kissed her on the forehead.

"We're home, I think," he said softly as she stirred.

"My gosh," she rubbed her eyes, "I really flaked out. It was the wine—it had to be."

As she pulled away, he growled, "It was the company—admit it. I'm about as exciting as a two cent stamp. Say, that is your car, isn't it." He was looking at a battered blue Pontiac.

"Yep, that's Sophie."

"Sophie?"

"I name all my cars. Don't you?"

"No. Why?"

"Sentimental, I guess."

"Tell me. How many have you had?"

"Sophie is number three."

"Who were the other two?"

"Doozie, an 'after the war re-tread', just died—old age. Then came Stud, a snazzy Studebaker. He didn't last long. Now I have Sophie and she's pure delight."

"Yeah, if you say so. (He looked once more at Sophie's beat-up exterior.) What was Stud's problem? I rather like that name."

"You would."

"Couldn't perform, right?"

"Bullseye."

"Geez, you're a trip, you know that."

"Just sentimental. (She thought, if I weren't you wouldn't be sitting here.) Want those cookies now?"

"Sure. That's all that kept me awake on the long drive." (Don't I wish, he thought.)

She slipped on her shoes, handed him her keys and they walked to her door.

The rain had completely stopped and everything smelled so fresh and clean as they stood in front of the large frame home. With its gingerbread trim and cupola rising from the top of the third floor, Sam felt almost as though he were living in another time.

She saw his eyes taking in the view. "It's a lovely old home, isn't it?"

"It's a piece of work, all right. You don't see too many like this anymore. How many apartments are there?"

"There's mine and one on the third floor. My landlady lives here on the first floor and rents out two rooms. I'll miss her. She's a delight!"

As he followed her up the steps, he couldn't help notice how wet her hose had gotten from their Memorial tour. "Penny, it looks as though you've been wading in the pool."

"You noticed?" (Why am I not surprised, she thought.)

"Are your feet cold?"

"No, just wet."

As they stepped into her dark apartment, she stooped over to pull off her pumps. This sudden movement on her part was unexpected and he bumped into her posterior almost knocking her forward onto the floor. He caught her by the waist just as she was going down, and spun her around.

He pulled her to him. "Sorry babe, that was unintentional. This isn't." And his lips began moving back and forth across hers in a teasing motion before settling squarely on her upturned mouth.

At last he gently released her, but their eyes never lost contact. God, no woman ever quite got to Sam like Penny and they were on a collision course from day one, and he knew it. She made no pretense when it came to her sensual lure—it was just there.

He could feel her body trembling against his, but she didn't pull away. Once again, his lips found hers, then moved to her eyelids, to a warm space behind her ears, and back again to her mouth. She received him willingly and nuzzled against his neck. If there was such a thing as sweet misery, this had to be it. With her arms still around his neck, but her head pulled back so that she looked straight into his eyes, she said, "God Sam you really try my will power like no one that I've ever met. Why?"

Although he didn't release his hold, his next words cut right into her. "Why? You know why, damn it, I like the feel of you in my arms. You bring out the best in me. You always did."

She smiled. "I'm that good, huh?"

"You're terrific," he whispered close to her ear. "Isn't it time I pulled that zipper down," and his hands moved toward the center of her back.

"It goes only one way," she teased, as she slowly pulled away, visibly shaken, and moved toward the kitchen. She flipped on the overhead light and after taking a few minutes to compose herself, called out,

"How about a cup of coffee with your cookies—Okay?"

He took off his coat and rolled up his cuffs. She kept this apartment too darn hot for him. "Yeah, sure that's fine."

She had the most of her cookies on a big dish, along with coffee on the table between them. As she bit into the second cookie, she asked with some trepidation, "Sam the last time I saw you, I think we had only a couple of hours together. And if I remember correctly, we did little talking 'cause you had just separated from Connie and weren't in the mood for conversation. It should be old news by now—want to tell me? I've always heard there's two sides when a couple splits, but what do I know."

There goes the cigarette again. He seems to need that lift when discussing his marriage.

"There's two sides all right, mine and Sam Boyer's." (He was bitter.)

"Are you sure you're ready to hear my disillusionment regarding so-called wedded bliss?"

"I asked because I wanted to hear."

"Well, when I returned right after the war—remember I saw you briefly. I think you were at the Sun then and I had already met Connie." (Oh Penny remembered—that's all she heard on that visit—Connie, Connie, and more Connie.) "She was also a military brat so we had much in common, I thought. I met her father overseas. He was a captain of a batallion that I served with for about nine months. He was 'Old Army' and about ready to retire when we got into the war. One of the greatest *soldiers* that I've ever met; however, not one of the greatest fathers. He had two daughters. Well, I was destined to fall in love with the older one—at first sight. Connie was just everything that I thought the perfect woman should be. You know me Pen—I wouldn't have settled for second best. You saw her picture— she was a real looker. She put up with my moods. All the guys returning, including me, had moody periods. None of us returned without some scars—emotional as well as physical. But we found 'the gold ring' and fell madly in love. We could have gone off half cocked and gotten married immediately—so many of the guys did, you know. We waited and took our time getting to know each other." He lit his second cigarette and Penny filled his coffee cup.

"We knew we'd be getting married. We talked of it many times. Of course, then we got playing around and had to move the wedding date up. She wanted a big wedding, but we decided to tone it down some after we realized she was pregnant. Even then, her family implied it was my fault. So you can see, our beginning was a little rocky. Needless to say, my family wasn't too overjoyed either when they found out. I have two sisters and I wasn't setting a very good example. Regardless, we got along real well for that six and a half months before Cal arrived. When her family got bossy and pushy, I just let it go —'cause I knew my next assignment sure as hell wasn't going to be close to family. And it wasn't! Remember I got a good deal with the Globe. Well, immediately I was bombarded with criticism for taking their daughter and their only grandchild so far away. That old record about moving around all their lives and now wanting to settle down and enjoy their family. I wasn't about to suggest that they come there to live 'cause secretly that was one of the reasons that I chose the Globe. Well, they worked on Connie and she gave me a fit and she knew for sure that I could get a position on a local paper. (She was right, too.) But I knew sure as my name was Sam Boyer, that the marriage wouldn't last if I had to marry the whole family to have Connie and Cal. In the end, she went with me. But from the time we settled in, she didn't like anything about the place. And I can't go in to details here 'cause I'd put you to sleep again if I listed all her complaints. Between her going to Illinois to visit and their coming to Boston, our lives were constantly on a merry-go-round. My family also wanted their share of visits. Finally, I got nasty and told her that I couldn't afford all those trips since I was working on my Master's at the same time. Do I need to go any further? The last knock-down, count to ten fight, came when she wanted to go to her cousin's wedding in Florida. She had just been to see her parents two weeks before, and now wanted to go gallivanting to Florida. She said not to worry that her parents would send her train fare. Well, that's when it hit the fan. I'll tell you Pen I was so damn mad—not only was I studying my balls off —she kept casting it up to me that I had tried to alienate her from her family ever since we were married and she'd about had it, and of course, in the heat of the argument, I told her that made two of us. So after her Florida trip, she didn't come back. She'd call and get teary on the phone and try coaxing me to come to Illinois to live. But I had made a decision that if she didn't love me enough to live with me, then it was best that she live with her family." His eyes got misty then. "But I sure miss my son—Oh Lord, ho, I miss him. You see, it doesn't matter that both families blame the split on me, that I can live with—but in order to stay with my son should I have given in and moved back to Illinois to please my wife and her family. I always come up with the same answer—she didn't really love me or it wouldn't have mattered. So you see there's only one side, that's mine."

"Bullseye," she said and pointed at him.

He looked at his watch, and said "I'm out of here, before the landlady kicks me out." Sighing, he stood up, rolled down his sleeves, and picked up his coat.

"Sam you never did tell me where you're staying, and I'd like to know."

He smiled. "That sounds encouraging. I'm at the Best Western down the road a few miles. I'll call you in the morning." As he worked his arms into his coat, and stifled a yawn, she thanked him for dinner and a lovely evening.

At the door, he turned, pulled her to him for one last lingering kiss, "You're quite a woman."

"I try. (out of breath) Good night and drive carefully."

It took her a long time to get to sleep that night. Just this morning she was planning on packing—a rather boring day, you might say. Then the door bell rang and who was standing there—Sam Boyer. Once he married, she definitely decided that should be the end of their visits. Of course, when he showed up for a few hours several years ago, it was to tell her the marriage was over. That time was spent with him crying on her shoulder. It was obvious that he was already missing his son. Since she was into a heavy romance at the time, she actually welcomed his *whirlwind* appearance. It saved explanations which would have been necessary. But she doubted seriously that she would see him again. What did she know? He was back!

She rolled over again and pulled the cover up to keep out the noise, then she realized it was her telephone. She squinted at the clock. It was 10. She reached over, and a sleepy "hello" came out.

"Penny?"

"Yes."

"It's me, Jason. Gee, I hope that I didn't get you awake."

"No."

"Just wondered if we're still on for tonight. I tried to get you last night but you must have been out."

"Yes, we're still on. What time should I be ready?"

"Well, would you like to go to that little Chinese place before we go to the film."

"Sure, I'd like that. Since the film begins at eight, we'd better leave here around six, Okay."

"Fine with me. I'll see you at six. Go back to sleep."

Penny was rather looking forward to the film which was produced by NACA regarding astronauts, space, and the moon landings. And she truly did enjoy Jason's company. He wasn't looking forward to any serious involvement. He was one of those college freaks—always going to school. This time it was for his doctorate. In fact, compared to Sam, his love-making came across as an afterthought. The only time he held her hand was when they stepped off the escalator. Anyway, they always had fun together. She had met Jason through another NACA scientist whom she had dated for almost a year and there were times when she still wondered if she shouldn't have accepted Tim's proposal. He'd had everything (sort of like Sam's Connie) and she knew Mom and Papa liked him. She took him home for Thanksgiving, and although they never pressured her one way or the other concerning her male friends, she sensed that he had made a big hit with them. When she announced that it was over between them—her parents seemed surprised, but accepted without comment. They knew about Sam since he existed as far back as college. They also understood it was just friendship—rather long-lasting, since it covered about 15 years. She remembered when she'd told them that Sam had gotten married their remark was "Well if you're happy for him, we are too."

Not many kids grow up with close ties to their parents to the extent of Penny's. And when they made that comment regarding Sam's marriage she got the impression they felt Penny's feelings were stronger than friendship, but of course that had been years ago. Her parents, especially her papa, were very perceptual. Even now it was difficult for Penny to assess her feelings truthfully for Sam Boyer. No man had ever excited her the way he could, but she also had enough sense to know that Sam didn't look on her as marriage material. He was a very complex personality with great bitterness now toward the institution of matrimony. Sometimes she came so close to chucking all her principles and giving in to Sam's desires—it was frightening. However, she gave herself enough credit to know that she'd be the loser in the end. She must have dozed off, 'cause she remembered telling Daisy to hurry up that it was time for her to walk down the aisle. Penny couldn't find her. Daisy suddenly appeared and pushed her friend toward the altar and said it's you not me, silly. Papa was waiting to marry her. Then she heard this loud bell. It was the phone.

"Hello."

"Good morning sleepy head. And don't tell me you're not still in bed. I can tell that 'Hello', and you're lying in bed."

"All right—so you've got ESP. I bet you haven't been up too long yourself, wise guy."

"That's where you're wrong. I've had breakfast, shaved, showered, and I'm heading out for an interview. So there! It looks as though I'll be here until Sunday. So get out your date book and mark me in where you have any blank spaces."

"Okay, hold on a minute. Ready? Today—12:30–5:30 p.m; Friday 7:30–9 a.m., 6–7 p.m., Saturday—(She could hear him laughing.) Sam you're not marking this down."

"All right lover girl, you left off tonight so I'm assuming that's out."

"Right. The rest of the time you're here, I'll be awaiting your pleasure."

"Yeah, promises, promises," he grumbled.

"Come again?"

"I'd like to."

"You're incorrigible."

"Yes, can we at least have lunch together today. Your date's tonight, right?"

"Why?"

"Somehow I knew it was time for 'why' to enter the conversation. Why you're going with that guy from NACA tonight, I don't know. Why you should have lunch with me is simply because we enjoy each other's company and if it goes over four years again, we'll leave so much conversation untouched."

"You win!" I'll fix lunch—don't dress, and make the conversation interesting."

"I'm wild about all three suggestions—especially the one in the middle."

"Remind me never to mention the Virgin Islands in your presence. See you around noon, Lover Boy." She hung up the phone and laughed to herself as she remembered her dream when his call came. Geez, she thought, who was standing at the altar. I'll never know!

At 12:45 p.m. her doorbell rang. She had pulled a matching slack suit from a box she had already packed, glanced in the mirror, wet her lips, and opened the door.

He thrust his arm in with a florist box. "My apology for the language I used earlier with a lady, but must admit that I've always wanted to visit the Virgin Islands." (That mischievous smile curved his lips.)

"Oh Sam! Sometimes I'd like to take a poke at you, and then other times . . . Why did you buy me flowers? Guys don't do that anymore."

"Guys don't, but gentlemen do." He made an exaggerated bow from the waist.

Her fingers were nervous as she untied the ribbon. There were one dozen beautiful long-stemmed red roses. Her eyes shined and her whole face glowed. No one had ever given her such beautiful flowers. In fact, a few tears seeped through and she was terribly embarrassed.

"Geez, they're beautiful. You shouldn't have, but I thank you for each one." She threw her arms around his neck and gave him a wet kiss on the cheek.

He took off his jacket and threw it across the chair. "Well, I didn't know you'd get so gushy. I got 'em half price—red isn't in right now."

He followed her to the kitchen as she hunted a container. "I only had two vases and they're packed, but I'll use wine carafes," she said as she pulled out some pans and dishes to get to the carafes. She placed six in each one, and arranged the fern accordingly. "Oh, they are so pretty." She carried one into the living room and the other she placed in the middle of her dinette table.

He was so pleased with himself. No one had ever made such a fuss over his flowers before.

When they sat down to the soup, salad, and sandwiches that she'd prepared for each of them, her first question was "How did your interview go?"

"Okay, I guess," as he took a big bite from his sandwich. "I believe that I'd prefer working here to New York and that seems to be the alternative on the east coast in this television media. I'm not getting my hopes up. I do have two other interviews scheduled. Of course, I'm not sure at this point if I'd work behind the scenes or in front of the camera, and it really wouldn't make any difference. I'd just like to try my hand at writing in TV. Again, Pen, I do want to apologize for my innuendos in our phone conversation. There was no excuse for that kind of talk and I wouldn't blame you for being angry. You are a *lady*, and always have been in my presence, damn it. Oh, there I go again. I must blame it on the company I've been keeping lately, but that will be changing, too."

"Apology accepted. I know you well enough to realize that it's all talk because you know me well enough—Oh, well, heck you know what I mean."

"Yes, dear heart, I know you very well. Good lunch. You developed into quite a cook, and you got all gussied up for me." (His eyes took in her attractive outfit.)

"I cannot tell a lie. I thought rather than change twice today I'd wear for my luncheon date what I'm wearing for my dinner date."

"That was very good. That shade of blue is your color—it matches your eyes. Did I ever tell you that you have beautiful blue eyes."

"Sam let's not carry this apology to the extreme. You know that you don't have to keep throwing compliments my way. Too many in too short a time, and I'll suspect that you have ulterior motives."

"Women—never satisfied. I talk horny and I shouldn't, and now I'm being complimentary and I shouldn't. What can I do to please you?"

"Just stay my friend as you have for 'lo these many years. You have a way of bringing me up when I'm down, and I don't want that to change."

"Come here and sit on my lap. You know you gave me another lead line again, but my lips are sealed."

She walked around the table and sat on his lap. He kissed her again and again. "That ham sandwich tastes even better now and he licked his lips. Okay, what jobs do you have lined up for me to do?"

She began clearing off the table, and suggested that they take a walk first since it was such a lovely day.

"Good idea," he said and began helping her with the dishes. (He dried a few glasses before excusing himself.)

They walked for almost an hour and talked for just about that long, too. He had a habit of running his fingers through his straight hair when he became involved with his subject, and somehow the hair stayed in place.

He'd fallen asleep on her sofa before they left and she studied his quiet features. Probably his mouth and white even teeth were his best features. (when he wasn't making those dirty cracks). He had a great voice for television, but would need to shape up on his appearance if he were in front of the camera. And of course that smile could melt an ice cube in January. Right now, he was doing a little snoring and she was hesitant about waking him, but if they were going to walk—they needed to get started. She blew in his face—his hand came up and stroked his cheek. She tried again by letting her hair tickle his nose. Once again his hand came up and rubbed his nose, the hand flopped back down again. Her last ruse was one too many. The ribbon was lying on the coffee table which had come off the florist box. She picked it up and delicately let it flow across his face when quicker than you could say hallelujah, his arms flew up and grabbed her and pulled her down on the sofa. She started laughing and the more she laughed, the more he continued tickling her.

"Oh Sam, you scared me. I thought you were still asleep. I should have known when the snoring slacked off." That got to him!

"Snoring," he growled, as he sat up. "I don't snore. I'm just a heavy breather."

"Okay heavy breather, are you ready for your exercise."

"Geez, I don't even remember falling asleep. Did I miss helping you with the dishes?"

"The whole nine yards. They're washed, dried, and put away. A fine mama's helper you make."

"I'm truly sorry," he said as he stood up flexing his arms and running in place. "Next time. I'm ready."

CHAPTER III

"Why did you decide to major in Journalism?"

"You."

"You're kidding."

"No, I'm not. If truth be known, I really wanted to be a doctor like Papa's sister, Miriam. "Are you still in love with Connie?"

"Am I what?"

"You heard me."

"Now it's my turn to ask why?"

"Curious I guess. If it's none of my business, tell me to butt out."

"No."

"Do you have any feelings for her at all?"

They were walking at a pretty good clip. Sam had on his walking shoes and he was putting them to good use.

"She's Cal's mother. That's it."

"I haven't known too many divorced couples. Does it take awhile to adjust? I know the last time we met—you flatly refused to discuss the entire situation."

"Sure it takes awhile. For all my bravado, I'm a pretty sensitive guy, or hadn't you noticed." He stooped, picked up a bottle cap and tossed it in the air. "Promise you won't laugh."

"Cross my heart." (and she did)

"There was a lot I liked about being married. I liked someone waiting on me when I got home at night. I liked waking up in the morning with someone beside me. I liked our private chats and even our minor disagreements. Gosh, I even enjoyed bathing Cal at times. But as time went on there seemed that there was more not to like. And now—Well, I just don't want to ever be hurt that way again." (He continued)

"You're the smart one. You haven't been hurt. By the way, one time you told me about the guy who wanted to marry you. I think you even took him home to meet your family. What happened there?"

"That was Tim Gresham, another NACA engineer. Slow down a little Boyer, I can't walk as fast as you." (She was out of breath and hurrying to catch up.)

"Sorry." he muttered.

"Oh yes, that was about three years ago. I really almost took the plunge that time. When I take a guy home—you know I'm getting serious. But I don't know, Sam, there was a spark missing. Maybe he was just too perfect. God, he had everything—a lot like your description of Connie. It's me I guess. My parents have the most wonderful relationship—even now. If I ever find the guy that I feel is right, really right for me—that spark should be there. If not, it'll be up to my brothers to supply grandchildren."

"Did they like this guy?"

"They seemed to. I said he was Mr. Perfect. What's not to like? But when I decided against accepting his proposal, they made no comment. They respected my decision."

"When are you taking me home to meet Papa and Mom?" He got a sheepish grin on his face.

"When I have something to report."

"Can't you just see me being a minister's son-in-law."

"Right now I can't see you ever being a son-in-law again, period."

"Pen you know me almost as well as I know myself."

"Sam how would you like to go to the zoo tomorrow?"

"Great, I'd love it. However, I'll have to call you after my interview. Is that all right?"

"Sure. I'm glad you came at this time. I never got a chance to take in all the wonders of D.C. 'cause I was always working and when I wasn't I took vacation away from the city.

Say, I do think we'd better head back. There's a few chores that I need to tend to before Jas comes."

"What's the guy's name?"

"Jason Watts."

"I knew a guy overseas named Watts. We used to always kid him about his high voltage. I was wondering." he said, rubbing his chin, "How's Jason's voltage?"

She was tickled. "Oh, not real high. I'd say tops about 130."

"At that rate, he'll never get home to meet the family."

"I think you might be right—but we enjoy each other's company. And when he's not studying for his doctorate, I'm his only extra-curricular activity."

"I'll just hop in the car that is if you can see yourself to the door."

"Your jacket."

"I knew there would be a reason for me to get back into your apartment."

She unlocked the door, and he picked up his jacket.

"Bye Pen. I'll call you tomorrow. We have a zoo date." He brushed her lips lightly, and continued to jog as he went dashing toward his car.

He drove to an Italian restaurant that he'd noticed earlier and had the chef fix him a pizza to go plus a couple bottles of beer and drove back to his motel. He propped his feet up and turned on the TV. After his shower, he sat on the bed and went over his interview forms for tomorrow. It was hard concentrating between the newlyweds next door and his thoughts of Penny. He didn't have the nerve to ask where they were going, but if she was going to wear her pant-suit, it couldn't have been too formal. If he was working on his doctorate, he was probably one of those "way out" characters who needed a shave. She seemed to take the relationship very lightly—you can bet Watts didn't. I think she called him a "chronic academic" whatever the hell that is. If a guy's into book learning, Penny Nagel's not the one to date. Why doesn't he go with a near-sighted bean pole. Oh well, he thought, why should I care anyway. It wasn't any of his business. He was looking over his reports for tomorrow, when he heard the newlyweds next door. They had ventured out only once—probably weak and had to get something to eat. He turned on the TV. He wasn't about to listen to bed springs and all those other sounds related to the mating game. My God, he'd paid extra for the TV and the reception was so poor it came across as a snow storm.

Geez, his mind went back to Penny. She was so darn much fun to be with. He was looking forward to going to the zoo tomorrow. He couldn't remember when he'd been to the zoo. He'd take her out to eat afterward. He laughed to himself. She really seemed to enjoy that white wine. He looked at his watch—10:10. He decided to call her.

"Hi. Is the Doc still there?"

"Yes. We just got here."

"Will he be there much longer?"

"I'm not sure. Why?"

"Oh God, that three-letter word again. Call me when he leaves. Do you have my number?"

"No, but I can get it. Thanks for calling."

"Sure." (click)

He tried the radio. Wouldn't you know they were playing one of Frankie's favorites, "My One and Only Love."

He heard a buzzing. Geez, he must of dozed off and it was his phone.

"Hello."

"I knew it. You were asleep, but I was afraid if I didn't call you'd think he spent the night." (She laughed)

He glanced at his watch—11:35. "Well, he practically did—it's almost Friday."

"Are you always so fussy when you first get awake?"

"Who's fussy—concerned is more like it."

"Sam, I'm a big girl. You don't need to worry."

"Did you enjoy your evening?"

"Yes."

"Better than last night."

"No."

"Serious."

"Yes, I'm serious. Just as much, but not better." (That'll fix him)

Damn, he thought, she had a smart mouth.

"What did *you* do?" she asked.

"Are you ready for this? I watched a snow storm on TV that I paid extra money for and listened to newlyweds next door humping up and down."

She laughed so loud, he had to hold the phone away from his ear.

"I'm glad you're enjoying it. I didn't."

"Are you sure they're newlyweds?"

"God, you can tell 'em a mile away. And if you say *why*, I'll hang up."

"That never entered my mind. You're becoming paranoid. About tomorrow, do you have any idea when you'll get here."

"Why?"

"I knew it. Well, I have some errands to take care

of and won't get back here until approximately
11:30."

"Suppose I call when I get back to the motel. I'll
want to change clothes, and by the way, we'll get
lunch on the run—so don't eat."

"Okay. Good night. I'm kind of bushed after that
long walk today."

"Was it the walk or your date?"

"Good night Sam." (She said icily.)

"Good night, Pen. Sweet dreams." (click)

Why did he do that to her? He knew better. The
sweet dreams was an after-thought 'cause she
sounded annoyed with his last question. And why
not. It was uncalled for and not very kind. Damn! He
was acting like a jealous teen-ager. He got out his
papers again and hoped he would now be able to
concentrate. The newlyweds had finally called it a
night. But now his thoughts were on a nasty streak
and a bad mouth which had targeted Penny, and he
didn't know why. Tomorrow first thing he'd apologize again.

Penny hadn't slept well. As for sweet dreams—bah
humbug. For some reason this morning she felt the
need to indulge in some self-pity. Next Saturday she
would have her final date with Jason before leaving
the area. In a couple of days Sam would be gone, for
who knows how long this time, and the following
week she would begin a new job. Well, that's what
she wanted, so why this morbid mood. Maybe it was
time for the horror pads. She laid down the paper as
she went to answer the phone.

"Hi. Am I too early?"

"No." She took another whiff of her roses.

"No sweet dreams?"

"I'll never tell."

"Not even me."

"Especially not you."

"You sound down. Is it that time of the month?"

(Damn him) "How did your interview go?"

"It's hard to tell. I tried to behave. I think they liked me. Just one more of these damn interviews to go—then I can go back to being Sam Boyer again."

"They're crazy if they let you get away."

"I'll take you along on my next interview." (He continued.)

"Is it Okay if I come over now? I can hear those monkeys rattling their cages."

"I'm yours for the rest of the day."

"If I'm late it's because I was caught for speeding. See you soon."

"I'll hold you to that."

She checked her make-up—ran a comb through her hair again, and wished for the umpteenth time that her darn jeans hadn't shrunk. The label said pre-shrunk, but that's just not true. (She could be a little swollen.) Oh well, she must remember not to stoop. Geez, she thought, when she heard the doorbell, he really could have a speeding ticket. He came in waving a white handkerchief.

"Sam, my Lord, you're surrendering. Why?"

"No, this is a flag of truce."

He looked so darn good in his jeans and Army jacket, but he was comical.

"I made a nasty comment on the phone last night and I'm apologizing—again." When she looked puz-

zled, he realized that it wasn't the 'cause of her low
morale. (Must be the time of the month after all.)
"You know when I suggested why you might be
tired."

"Oh Lord, that. I just consider the source."

He threw his jacket on the sofa. Came over to
where she stood, and took her into his arms, and
kissed her. As always, he took her breath away and
turned her legs to jelly. And, as always, she gave back
to him what he wanted.

"I missed you last night. It was lonely," he said, as
they came up for air, "and since we can't neck at the
zoo, I'm getting an early start."

Slowly she pulled away. His one hand was about to
pull in her rump.

"Don't give me that lonely stuff. You were jealous,
admit it."

"Me—jealous." He threw up his hands.

"Yes, jealous of the newlyweds next door." She
turned around to face him and started laughing. She
pointed her finger at him. Bullseye!"

"Well, it did make it most difficult to concentrate,
plus the fact you and Jason were making-out in front
of my roses."

"Would you like some coffee before we go?"

He lit a cigarette, and went over to his chair.

"No thanks. I'd rather hear about your dreams."

She went to the kitchen and brought herself a cup
of coffee into the living room where she sat on the
sofa. "My dreams are off limits." (no laughter this
time)

"Subject closed. You look a little pale. Sure you
feel all right?"

"Sam, I'm fine."

"There's a great deal of walking involved while touring the zoo."

"All right—you win. It is that time of the month, but walking doesn't bother me. It never has and we are going to the zoo. Satisfied."

(Geez is she ever touchy.) He went over to the sofa, sat down, and put his arms around her shoulders pulling her to him. "You're really a trooper, you know that." He kissed her on the forehead.

"Trooper?" Her voice raised an octave higher. "Come on Sam, let's not get icky over such normal facts of life. You're out of character."

"Whew! You know what I think," he said, withdrawing his arm, "I think I'm in for a l-o-n-g day."

"I'm counting on it," she said as she walked to her closet and withdrew her jacket handing it to him.

His eyes followed her as she moved away. She had the sexiest little ass this side of the Potomac, and was glad when she turned her back to fit her arms into her coat.

"I studied the map, so I think I can find the zoo."

"Good."

"You trust me."

"Do I have a choice?"

"Penny, I met a guy this morning that I've known for years. He invited me to a dinner and dance at his club tomorrow night. I'd like you to go with me. How about it?"

"Gosh, we've never done the big time. Do you think we can handle such a challenge?"

"If you're game, I'm willing to give it a try."

"Is it formal?"

"Semi."

"So I just wear my Sunday dress, but show a little cleavage."

"Sounds good to me. That means you'll go."

"I perform a lousy rumba, but if I carry one of your roses in my mouth, I might be coaxed into the tango."

"I just learned to jitterbug and that's been out for 10 years, so you're safe on that score."

"What time is my date coming?" He whistled.

"Strike that. What time will my date be calling for me?"

"I'll let you know. I must call the guy tonight and confirm so he can make reservations. I knew him overseas, Hal Conner, he's with the State Department—married and settled. I've never met his wife, *Marilyn*, I believe."

"Sam, are you sure we didn't just pass the entrance to the zoo?"

"No, I'm not sure—I was in the middle of an introduction. Why do I get lost when you're with me. When I'm alone, I have no problems."

She laughed. "That's because I shake you up."

"Ho Ho! There it is right up ahead."

They sat on a bench and ate foot-long hot dogs and drank a coke before starting out. Penny had to have a bag of popcorn to nibble on while strolling from cage to cage. They watched the monkeys make love. (This must have been the season) The lions roared at them, and the elephants coaxed for popcorn. (They didn't get any.) There was a cool breeze and both zipped up their jackets. Every step of the way was a delight. They would both remember their day at the zoo for many years to come. At regular intervals, Sam was very solicitous in asking Penny if she was tired. They did sit down to rest twice and Sam went to purchase each a bag of peanuts.

She saw a side of Sam today that she didn't know existed, and it gave her a good feeling. She knew how very considerate he must have been with Connie during her pregnancy. And for the first time, even though her heart and mind fought against it, she realized that this smart-mouth journalist, with the straight hair and dazzling smile was the guy who created the spark, and instead of making her happy —she was saddened.

As they walked away from the camels after almost three hours, Sam said, "Babe, I think that's it. We've had enough animal kingdom for one day. What do you say?"

"Since they won't let me ride the camel, I've decided you're right. Let's start toward the car—which is—Oh, we're lost again."

(In situations such as this. You must think positive.)

As he threw the bag in the trash basket, after tossing the last peanut in his mouth, he said, "Oh no, just follow your tour guide and he'll have you out of here in no time. If you're tired, I can carry you piggy back."

"Sam I know you too well, so I won't even jest, or you'd have me on your back before I could say hallelujah."

They left the zoo singing a song about a monkey wrapping his tail, or something, off-key, but full of spirit.

Dusk was beginning to turn into night before Sam maneuvered the car on the direct route into Alexandria. He glanced over at Penny who was unusually quiet and saw that her eyelids were closed. He hoped she was having sweet dreams. When he had to brake quite suddenly at the next block for a red light, her eyes popped open.

"Sorry I got you awake. It wasn't intentional, I assure you."

"I can't believe I fell asleep again. Darn, I'm worse than an old lady. You're not lost, are you?" she asked, stretching.

"You have no faith in me at all—I am *not* lost, and we're soon home. Are you hungry or do you want to wait awhile and I'll go get some take-out food."

"Do you like scrambled eggs, ham, and bagels"

"Sure, but I don't want you cooking tonight."

"*We're* cooking tonight. I suggest that it be a joint effort just so you won't feel as though you're imposing."

"Would you believe your suggestion has merit. I made the best scrambled eggs in our battalion."

"All right—you're on."

An hour later, both in their stocking feet, both with their assigned tasks, were assembling a meal fit for a king.

Penny set a lighted candle on the dinette table along with her carafe of roses, and they ate scrambled eggs, hickory smoked ham, bagels, and a dish of fruit cocktail.

"Your entree is superb Mr. Boyer. I must have your recipe."

"Miss Nagel I have never tasted such succulent fruit. However do you keep it so fresh?"

"Lean over," and she beckoned with her forefinger, as she popped a grape into his mouth. He licked his lips. "Now that is vine-ripened."

He poured his third goblet of wine and decided on a toast. He filled her goblet which almost emptied the bottle and said, as they touched glasses, "to a most wonderful day at the zoo, to a most wonderful meal, and last to the divine company."

"I'll drink to that," and that's the last toast for me. I'm not a drinker and I've had my quota of wine."

She washed and he dried. She decided to reward him with a kiss. He was backed up to the counter, and needless to say was shocked by her brazen action, but more than willing. Her arms went around his neck, and as her lips came in to meet his, she said, "Sam thanks for today." Their mouths came together for their sexy kiss.

"Hm-m-m, I love the taste of that wine coming from your lips. Let's do it some more."

"You're right," she whispered, licking her lips, "that's tasty."

It was awhile before they pulled apart. This time Sam drew back first and Penny could tell why. Even though she was very relaxed, she knew an arousal and Sam had a "doozie."

After a period of silence, Sam asked if he could put some records on the record player.

"Oh I'm sorry, I've already packed them, but there is a station on the radio that plays music, called *Music for Swinging* or something." As she sashayed over to the radio and stooped over to adjust the dial, he thought he could hardly stand it.

"Get comfy," she said.

God, that was almost impossible. He got out a cigarette and propped up his feet on the coffee table. The strains of *Close to You* floated through the room as Pen came back, sat beside him on the sofa, and propped her feet up aside of his. She had taken off her socks, and he noticed what pretty feet she had. Crazy thing about feet—some were ugly and some were pretty. He had never seen her feet before. All these years he had known her and had never seen her barefeet.

"Why did you take off your socks?"

"I know it sounds silly, but I love the feel of the rug on my barefeet."

"You probably like to walk in the sand, too."

"Oh, I love it."

Penny looked around her living room, normally very clean and everything in its place. Now for the first time since Sam's arrival, she was embarrassed. She had taken her curtains and pictures down, and although her furniture wasn't expensive or the most attractive, she had kept it polished. Her book shelves were empty and her record player was packed.

"Sam I want to apologize for the appearance of my apartment. Actually, I'm quite a good house-keeper. Please excuse the dirt and cobwebs."

"You're crazy, you know that. Why would you clean a place when you're moving next week."

"My feeling exactly," she said, emphatically. "Once it's empty, I'll give it the full treatment."

"Okay now sit back and relax," he said, as he

reached down and began rubbing her feet. She jerked slightly.

"Does that bother you?"

"Not as long as you don't touch my soles. There I'm very ticklish."

"Not to worry, my dear, when it comes to podiatry, I'm an expert." He continued rubbing her feet. "Doesn't that feel good?"

"Oh yes."

"Move down toward the end of the sofa and put your feet on my lap."

As he moved toward his end of the sofa, she lifted her legs up so that her calves and feet rested on his lap.

He pushed her jeans up to her knees, and began massaging her lower legs and feet.

"Oh-h that feels good. Your hands are so soothing. Have you done this before?"

"Oh yes. When my wife was pregnant—she enjoyed my massaging her legs and feet. They'd swell and ache near the end. I guess that I felt it might feel good to you at this particular time."

She knew her memories of these days alone with Sam would have to last a long, long time.

"What are you thinking?" he asked, as he continued to rub her calves and the tops of her feet.

"What a pair of hands!"

"What a pair of legs!"

"Sam did I tell you that I've written a novel—Well, it's not really a novel. It still has many rough edges, but since you've already been published, would you be kind enough to review and evaluate my work."

"Is that the work which deals with your parents' life story?"

"Yes, well actually it started out as an edited version of Papa's experiences during WW I. He kept a diary the whole time, you know. It is most interesting. But after I got into it, I decided to go the whole way and write an entire story of Pen Nagel's life. I won't say anymore until you've read it. It will be my gift to them some day. I'm not seeking publication or recognition."

"Sure. Just give me the manuscript and I'll be happy to review and evaluate not that my recommendation is that valuable, but I really would like to read the story."

"Great! I'll give you a copy before you leave."

"Did you know that you basically have cold feet?"

"Why basically?"

"Because when I stopped rubbing, your little piggies chilled off."

"Sam you're tickling—now stop that."

"This little piggy went to market. You remember that," and he began jiggling each toe.

She was laughing and pulling her feet away. "I knew that massage bit was too good to last. Let me up. I'll go get my slippers."

"I'll get 'em. I have to make a necessary trip anyway."

"Thanks. They should be right beside my bed," she called as he strode toward the bathroom. "They're red."

He felt for the light switch and when he flipped the button, a small lamp went on beside her bed. He saw her slippers but spent a few minutes looking around. The room was very neat; however, you could tell she was preparing to move. There were boxes stacked along the wall. (He noted her shoes and socks on the floor.) Geez, those shoes were a rare vintage. The room smelled good—it smelled like Penny—tangy. On the bedside table was a framed picture. It had to be her parents. Good looking couple, young, too. Her bureau still had her brush and comb, and assorted bottles, then he spied a little picture of some guy sticking on the edge of the mirror. He decided that was Jason—not bad either, especially for a guy that studies all the time. He almost dropped her slippers when the phone rang—right in his ear as he stooped over.

After the second ring, he realized she picked it up in the living room. He walked slowly down the hall. He didn't want her to think he was trying to listen (even though he was). She was laughing into the phone. He picked up the newspaper, hunted the sports page and looked interested, while listening to Pen's conversation. "I can't believe that. You should have told me. No, I'll be busy packing. Oh sure, I'll remember. See ya. Call first. Good night."

CHAPTER IV

"Put your feet up. Geez these things surely must keep your feet warm," he said, as he slipped them on.

He sat down again beside her on the sofa, and once more put his feet up beside hers on the coffee table.

"Sam you thirsty or hungry?"

"No, but hearing that phone ring reminded me I need to call Hal." He got out his wallet and fished around for a card. "Okay if I use the phone?"

"Sure, except calls to California."

"You're lucky this one is to Washington."

He dialed the number and waited. On about the fifth ring, a voice answered, "Conner residence."

"This is Sam Boyer calling Hal Conner. Hope this isn't a bad time. Good. Yes, there will be two of us.

Oh, we'll find it—7 p.m. Penny Nagel. Thanks. Goodbye."

"They wanted your name. Must check you out with the State Department."

She threw a pillow at him. "That was your second mistake."

"What was the first?"

"Asking me."

"I told him this morning that the Post got rid of you because of some shady deal, but if I got lucky maybe I could search out the truth."

He was laughing as he sat on the sofa and she was going at him with both fists. "Sam Boyer, I'll never trust you again. You blew my cover."

He captured both arms and pulled them around his middle. His lips found hers and they clung together. His hands held her face close to his, and as he lifted his lips from hers, he whispered, "Did I really blow your cover?"

As she opened her mouth with some wise remark, his lips covered hers again and again. He pulled her down so that she was looking down into his eyes. She did a little moving on his face. She kissed his eyes, under his ears, and then slid back again to his lips. Tremors from his torso transferred into hers, and she could feel his hands moving up under her shirt.

"Sam."

"I know. I'm just rubbing your back—what's wrong with that. You're playing hopscotch on my face and I'm supposed to keep my hands in my pockets."

"What time is your interview tomorrow?"

"Pen can you move over a little. I know that looks sexy with you on top and all, but I've got a problem."

She slid down beside him on the inside. "Sorry. That better?"

"Not really, but with you it's as good as it gets. My interview is at 10 a.m."

"Why 10?"

"So the guy can screw up your whole morning. You see they come into work at 9:30. Then they shuffle papers around on their desk. Then it's time for coffee with their secretary. After a trip to the john, the secretary announces the 10 o'clock appointment has arrived. You go in the office, and the guy says, 'Have a chair be with you in a minute'. That gives you time to try and look what's lying on his desk. He probably went to the john again and washed his hands. When he steps back in, he says, 'Sam Boyer, war correspondent', and you stand up and shake his hand. Then he buzzes little Miss Efficient, and she trips in with your file. He opens it up, and says, 'Let's see'. And you know damn well he's read it at least once and probably twice. By that time it's almost 10:30 and your whole morning's screwed up."

Penny was laughing so hard that tears were running down her cheeks and she needed to blow her nose.

"Where's that hankie you waved at me today?"

Well, when he went to get it out of his pocket, he got too close to the edge of the sofa and off he went onto the floor.

"Sam look out you're falling on the floor." When she grabbed for him, he had such a startled look on his face (if he'd been hurt, she couldn't have stopped laughing). Just about that time she felt a spring pop up from under the sofa, which threw her off balance and she flew on the floor, too. They were both laughing hysterically now, and Penny never did get the hankie, and she was trying to thank Sam for breaking her fall.

"Sam you're such a gentleman," she finally got the words out, "you've made my fall so soft."

"Yeah," he laughed, "and in your condition that's," more laughter, "damned important."

She finally found his handkerchief under the sofa, wiped her tears and nose, and then repeated the action again. They didn't check the time, so who knows how long they lay on the floor laughing. Finally they got on their feet.

"Well, I've heard of 'a roll in the hay', but this is ridiculous."

"Sam, are you hurt?"

He was grabbing his ribs and then his jaw.

"I'm checking. You've got the sharpest elbows this side of the Potomac. I think you've fractured my jaw."

"Oh God no," and she had laughed.

He kept moving his jaw around, and then turned to her and pointing to his cheek, said, "Kiss it right here and make it all better."

"Oh you—you're impossible."

"Well, it always worked with my mother."

"Sam I think that sofa's had it. Did you know a spring shot up and shot me right through the air?"

"Oh I know all right."

He felt around the sofa and found the errant

spring. "I think this baby just couldn't handle our activity. Is this yours or did it come furnished?"

"That's one of my sentimental pieces. I've had it ever since college."

"Well I think it just died. Pen, I'm serious, I wouldn't pay to move this sentimental piece one more mile."

"Now I'm thirsty. I'm going to your fridge."

"Me, too."

He pulled out a beer. She pulled out a coke. They walked back into the living room and sat on the floor resting their backs against the sofa.

"Before the excitement, you were giving me a blow by blow description of your interview."

"You don't drink beer?"

"Nope. Don't care for it."

"You seem to keep it in your fridge."

"Well, I try to be a good hostess."

"Jason drinks it, too, eh."

"On occasion, yes."

"Is that his picture in your bedroom—the one sticking on the mirror? I noticed it when I went for your slippers."

"Yes."

"He's not bad. Not at all how I imagined him."

"Glad you approve."

He took another swig of beer. "That was him on the phone, wasn't it?"

"Yes."

"Are you in love with him?"

"No."

"Is he in love with you?"

"Good Lord, Sam, what is this—twenty questions.

I'm sure you have a girl in every city plus a few over-seas and know more about the female anatomy than even I do."

"Is he in love with you?"

"This is my last answer. He thinks he is."

He burped and excused himself. She just excused herself.

When she came back from the bathroom, he was getting into his jacket. "Well, babe I'd better hit the road."

"What time should I be ready tomorrow night?"

"How about 6:30."

She walked him to the door. "We had a good time today, didn't we."

"We had a great time today. Thanks for the zoo, and breaking my fall from the sofa."

"Thanks for the brew and my candlelight meal. Oh hell, this is getting sickening. See you tomorrow night."

His lips brushed lightly over hers. The act was tender and thoughtful. Then suddenly he turned.

"Penny wait . . . my shoes."

She looked down and he was standing in the hall in his stocking feet.

"Well, jimeny, what did you do with your shoes."

"I thought I left them under my chair." (He was down on his hands and knees looking.)

"Your chair?"

"Well, it's where I always sit when I come in. It's where I should have stayed today." (he mumbled)

"They're out here," she called from the kitchen. "Remember you kicked them off before making your omelet."

She remembered her two stipulations when she purchased this dress for her farewell party at the Post. She'd told the clerk—no ruffles and no crinolines, but sexy. The clerk knew her job!

As she checked her full-length mirror for the last time, she was satisfied once again with the dress that had cost her big bucks. Penny wasn't a fashion expert, but her mom had always told her in black you're always in good taste. (Her mom did have a background of clothes knowledge.) Consequently, usually her special dresses were black, but this time royal blue won out. Penny knew the minute she saw it on the hanger—she had to have it. Her wardrobe was limited—an economic necessity, so each outfit was purchased with the knowledge that it would be worn on more than one occasion. She hoped tonight her attire would be accepted as excellent taste. From the waist up to the neck the see-through tulle covered the fitted bodice of a silk-like fabric. The soft tulle covered both arms down to the wrist. The skirt had a flare from the waist, however no crinolines. She remembered the little clerk's comment, "Honey that should win him over." Pen didn't want to win anyone; she just wanted to make sure that she didn't embarrass Sam when meeting his friends. (Jason had certainly liked it.) At the last minute just as she heard Sam at the door, she decided to slip on her old sneakers. (remembering his comment)

Sam took her breath away—for sure. She had never seen him so well groomed. This Conner must really be some guy, she concluded, as she invited Sam into the living room.

"Wow! Is this the same guy that left here last night in his stocking feet."

He was already to comment, when at that minute he noticed her "sneaks" and burst out laughing. "Pen, what a match. My God, they're perfect."

They both laughed again. As their laughter subsided, Penny left for a tissue.

"Have a chair. I need to wipe 'funny' tears again."

When she re-entered the living room, she brought her coat and had changed her shoes. "Hope you don't mind. Those sneakers really weren't a 'perfect' match."

"Penny you'll be the prettiest lady there, and I can only pray that you'll save me a dance." (He clasped his hands together and looked up toward the Heavens.) He continued.

"What did you do to your hair?"

"It's called Ava Gardner in dirty blond. I had it designed just for this bash. Do you like it?"

"Don't tell Sinatra, but Ava never looked this good. I almost forgot, here's a bottle of your favorite wine. What do you say we have a little toast before we go."

"Well thank you. First roses, then wine—Sam I'm overwhelmed. You open the bottle." They went to the kitchen.

Sam held up his glass and touched Pen's as he said, "To a memorable evening with my best girl friend."

"You're getting icky again."

"You're right."

"Why?"

"I'm just a nice guy."

"I think it's time to go and begin that memorable evening."

"After you."

"Do you know how to get there?"

"Sure. I studied the map."

"I liked the wine—that was very thoughtful."

"Now who is getting icky," he said as he opened the door.

Penny had a wonderful evening from the time they arrived until they pulled into the parking space at her apartment. She enjoyed Sam's friends. They weren't snobs. (She thought they might be.)

Their dancing went pretty well, too. As the evening progressed, they became more relaxed. They all joined in the Bunnie Hop and ended up with different partners. And that was fun, too.

Sam and Hal seemed to get along very well. Apparently they had shared some war experiences and enjoyed a special kind of rapport.

The last dance was at 12:30 a.m., and of course by that time she and Sam really had mastered the art of moving their feet in perfect harmony. In fact, they were so relaxed, he was doing a bit of necking on the dance floor. She was flustered, to say the least, when she felt his lips on her neck and then slip around on her lips. Naturally, she missed a step. That song didn't help matters either—*The Nearness Of You.*

"Sorry," she mumbled, "it's hard to concentrate on my dancing when you're . . ." His lips stopped her.

"Sam, someone might see you."

"Someone might hear you."

So she kept quiet, and he was happy doing his thing. She was as nervous as a catbird.

After one ring, she picked up the phone.

"Hello."

As she expected that rich baritone voice said, "Hello there. What you doing?"

"Lying here in bed waiting for your call."

"Wanted to let you know that I arrived back at the motel safely."

"I'm glad."

"You were worried?"

"I might have been."

"You sleepy?"

"No. Just thinking about what a wonderful time I had tonight. I liked your friends; I liked the food; I liked the music; and I liked the dancing—not necessarily in that order."

"And-d-d, how about your date?"

"He was delectable until he started smooching right on the dance floor."

"Oh you liked it."

"I did?"

"And after that?"

"After what?"

"Well, he was delectable up until that point, and after that."

"The fire's just beginning to subside."

He laughed. Oh Lord, what he wouldn't give to really explode a fire in her.

"It's your fault for looking so irresistible in that dress that matched your eyes with that deep V-neckline and the back out. Oh, I know it was covered with that netty stuff. Did you have me in mind when you bought it?"

"No."

"Well, I bet you took the scissors and cut that opening in the back down to your waist just so I could slip my hands through and feel the bareness underneath."

"No. The last time I wore it, there was no problem."

"You mean Jason let that opportunity slip by."

"He's a gentleman."

"And I'm not?"

She laughed. "Yeah, a gentleman with roving hands."

"What do you have on?"

"Now?"

"Yeah."

"A shirt. Why?"

"Just wanted to imagine what you look like lying there in bed. A shirt?" His voice pitched high.

"My night shirt. I'm not much on those see-through nighties. What are you wearing?"

"I'm not much on those see-through nighties either, so I just wear my shorts."

"Glad to hear it. I was afraid, knowing you, that you went bare bottom."

"Normally, I do, but not when having a conversation with you. Now another reason for my call. Are we still on for that movie tonight?"

"Oh, I hope so. It's *From Here To Eternity*. You know me, I always was great on movies. Did I ever tell you that my friend, Roberta, and I used to go every Saturday afternoon."

"No you didn't. But you really want to go this afternoon."

"Oh Lord," she looked at the clock—it really was already Saturday.

"You got a problem?"

"No. I just realized it was already Saturday. It sounds strange to say I'll cook you dinner tonight, but I will."

"I accept. Check when the show starts and call me. If I'm not in leave a message at the desk. Okay?"

"Sam, when did you say you were leaving?"

"Trying to get rid of me, eh."

"What else—this is getting to be a drag, you know. I feel as though I'm going steady."

"Fun, aint it?"

If he only knew, it was killing her. She was already dreading next week. This was the longest period that she'd ever spent with him, and God only knew how long it would be before she'd see him again.

"Oh, I think check-out time is eleven, so I'll probably head north after I get a bite to eat. I'm visiting my parents first, and then on to Illinois to see Cal. I sent her a wire yesterday. Were you planning a farewell party for me?"

"Something like that. Just wanted to know if I cook you a steak or a hamburger tonight. Farewell meals rate steak."

"Are you going to miss me?"

"Yes. I'll be able to get back to my packing."

"Flattery will get you nowhere. Did I just hear a yawn? Well, I can take a hint. Sweet dreams, Pen."

"Good night Sam."

*   *   *

They ate hot dogs and popcorn and a huge cup of
sodapop before going into the heavily attended
movie. Halfway through, Sam sought her hand. She
was conscious of his thigh brushing against her as he
sat with his legs spread apart. Most of the time there
was some smart alec making sounds during very
tender love scenes, but not today. In fact, Penny was
certain that Sam's grip tightened during one of the
choice love scenes on the beach between Burt Lancaster and Deborah Kerr. Once she looked over at his
profile in the semi-darkness and at that moment he
chose to look at her. She really couldn't put a name
to the look, but it wasn't his usual smug, egotistical,
or teasing stare, and for some reason she felt uneasy.

Until she requested that he stop at the bakery,
they were quiet on the way home. "What's your favorite pie?"

"Cherry."

"I might have known." (That was Papa's favorite
pie)

"What does that mean?"

"Forget it. Here's the bakery. It'll take me just a
few minutes." She hopped out before he could answer.

With his assistance, they set up her little grill on
the balcony. She put two potatoes in the oven,
tossed a salad, and gave him their steaks to put on
the grill. Since this was his last night—she went all
out. That morning she had run to the 5 & 10 and
bought some cheap candlesticks and blueberry can-
dles. Her roses had stayed remarkably fresh and with
half bottle of wine, their meal was a glorious success,
pretty, too.

He looked at her from across the candlelight and said, "Toast. Until we meet again, Pen, don't change."

She added, I won't if you won't."

"Deal." They hit their glasses together and downed the wine.

"I don't think I'll need my specs because I know this steak is done to perfection. I supervised the broiling."

As they finished their dinner topped off with cherry pie, Sam's comment was "You do indeed know how to prepare a delicious dinner. Thank-you Penny." He bowed very low swinging his napkin far out.

"Kick off your shoes and get comfy. I'll be there in a few minutes. Couldn't have done it without your help."

"I'll kick off my shoes, but I'm helping you. I may not pack boxes, but I'm an expert at dishes."

"What was it like in Korea?"

"You don't want to know Pen, but if you're really interested, I'll have a book coming out in about six months, called *38th Parallel: The Korean Conflict*, and I'll send you a copy. Which reminds me before I leave you promised me your manuscript."

"Oh you're far too busy to bother with it. Forget I even ask."

"No, please go get it for me. I want to read it. Maybe it will help me to better understand Penelope Nagel."

"Maybe." (she mumbled) She went into her bedroom and came out a few minutes later carrying the manuscript. "There's no rush and when you're finished just send it COD to the Lancaster New Era. Okay. Sam I really appreciate you're taking the time."

"Believe me, it will be my pleasure." He laid it by his jacket. "What do you usually do on Sundays," he asked, as he finished the last of the dishes.

"Nothing exciting by your standards. I go to church first. Later on in the day, sometimes I call Mom and Papa. The rest of the day, I do as I darn well please."

As they walked toward the living room, he said, "You're very close to your parents, aren't you."

"Yes."

"I don't trust that damn sofa. Can we just sit on the floor and talk.

"What you really mean Sam is we'll talk unless you can come up with a better idea."

"Pen, this is my last night. Don't you want to send me away happy?"

As she swung around to answer him, he caught her in his arms, and slowly removed the clip from her pony tail running his fingers through her shoulder-length hair. Very softly and close to her lips, he said, "It looks like the Ava Gardner look turned into the Debby Reynolds, but I like it either way." Then his lips found hers, and she knew that once again they were caught up in the web of sexual desire. His lips were warm and demanding, and her body trembled. When they came up for air, his eyes bore into hers. She had never seen him quite so intense.

Nervously, she began pulling away, as she said, "Don't you want to sit on the floor?"

"Not really, but I know that I have no other choice."

She went to her bedroom once again and came out with her old quilt. Sam was in the bathroom. She arranged it on the floor, so they could rest their backs on the sofa. She brought a college photo album with her which she felt he might enjoy looking at. (at least she hoped he would) He did!

Sam knew his parents loved him although they never had been demonstrative with their feelings. They were both northerners, and Sam had been around the world enough to know there was a difference between north and south when it came to warmth and passion. Furthermore, his father had been career military and lived through it. His mother was cool and reserved, rather stoic. She even looked the part, being tall and thin with sharp cheek bones. His two sisters Christy and Carolyn were happily married. In fact, he was already an uncle. Christy, three years younger than him, had become a teacher after graduating from Delaware University. She had married a year before Sam and had two kids. His younger sister had not attended college. Instead she had joined the WAVES and married a guy she'd met in the service.

As the miles grew that separated him from Washington, his expectations of what to expect upon his arrival would be just about the same as always—a handshake from his dad with a request to fill him in on his latest exploits and his mother waiting patiently behind for her traditional kiss on the cheek. If the sisters and brothers-in-law could make it, they'd come by to say hello. He'd only be there for a few days anyway—so why the big deal. But deep down inside, after hearing Penny talk so much about her family just once it would be nice to come home to a special kind of homecoming. Hank, the dentist brother-in-law, could take some time off, and Bill, with whom he shared a special rapport, could do likewise, but then his family would consider that rather frivolous.

He had stopped to eat and fill his gas tank, and with just 30 miles left—he was ready to land. His joints were getting stiff. God, he must be getting old, or Buffalo was moving further away.

He had called Pen to say goodbye but she must have been in church, 'cause there was no answer. He liked to imagine her reaction when she received the little heart-shaped pin he'd gotten her. He left her address and some money with the motel clerk to have it delivered. He hadn't read her manuscript yet, but he noted the title, *The Pen Nagel Story*.

Sam understood that Penny's book title, *The Pen Nagel Story*, was the story of her parents' life. Pen was her father's nickname which was derived from his three names Phillip Eugene Nagel. It was a name tagged on him as a little boy and stuck. On his trip to Illinois, he'd have a chance for some reading. Then he began wondering about his son, and really didn't know what to expect.

CHAPTER V

HE HAD told his mother that she needn't get up with him when two days later he'd be getting an early start to leave for Illinois, so he was shocked to find her in the kitchen when he came downstairs and smelled coffee brewing. Will wonders never cease, he thought.

"Well, son your visit was brief as always, but we did enjoy having you. If an offer comes through in Washington, you won't be too far away this time. Is there someone special there, or just better opportunities?"

"No one special, and you didn't need to get up."

"I wanted to. Give that little grandson of ours a hug and kiss. We certainly don't get to see him very often." (There was a hint of melancholia in her voice.)

"I know. I don't myself. However, if I land a job in D.C., this summer I'll make sure you see him."

"He must be about seven. Has she ever married again?"

"The last I heard she was engaged, so I'm sure by now she's married some guy who will stay close by her home. That's sure to satisfy her old man."

"Are you still in love with her?"

"Are you kidding?" (accompanied by a cynical laugh) Whatever gave you that idea. She killed that a long time ago."

"Well, you never found anyone else to marry."

"Why should I?" You must admit that I wasn't very successful at staying married," he said, as he buttered his second piece of toast.

She sat down across the table from him, and for the first time in many years, she seemed really concerned.

"Sam, I'd like to see you happily married. You have so much to offer a woman and you love children."

He laid his hand on hers, also for the first time in many years, and said, "I'm happy just the way things are. You have two daughters happily married. Marriage just isn't for everyone. You must admit my life style isn't the norm."

"Neither was your father's, but somehow we managed to hold a family together." (not always happy, she thought, but together)

As he used his napkin to wipe some crumbs away, he stood up, and thanked her for making his breakfast.

"I'll be staying at that same motel. Here's the

number." He handed her a card. "If I get any calls or mail from Washington that sounds important call."

Yes, she nodded, as she took the card.

He grabbed up his valise and headed out the door, kissing her on the cheek as he left.

He was always glad when that visit was over. Although this time it was more pleasant than usual. The old man actually seemed friendly and his mother getting up to fix his breakfast was quite an unexpected surprise. He chuckled to himself. Maybe they're getting mellow in their old age. (Yep, he figured the old West Point graduate had to be 62 this year).

Christy had made it a point last night to tell him that an old high school sweetheart was now a widow, since her husband had been killed in Korea. He hadn't thought about Allison for a long time. They had been an item way back. She was a cheerleader and he played football. The perfect pair! Then one night he tried to get fresh with her in the back seat of Herbie Denkel's car. Hell, if he remembered correctly, he'd only wanted a feel. She'd gotten very upset, and then he realized why. Allison didn't have the tits that everyone thought she had. In fact, they were hardly more than little bumps. What bothered him most was her misleading everyone into believing that she was really stacked. When he found out that gorgeous pair of knockers weren't the "real McCoy," he just lost trust in her, and he'd never felt the same about her after that.

Now his mind was on boobs and they brought to mind Penny. Oh, yeah, he'd learned a long time ago how you distinguish between the real and the artifi-

cial, and Penny's were real. That last night in her
apartment when she so cleverly got him interested in
looking at college year books while they sat on the
floor, he noticed! She had on a long, full skirt with a
white blouse. The blouse had some screwy kind of
buttons in the front and once when she reached over
him to get a book, didn't they get caught on the
front of his shirt. It probably wouldn't happen again
in a million years, but it happened to them. God, she
was so embarrassed her face got as red as a beet. He
had about decided that he'd have to take off his shirt
(over his head) when they finally became untangled,
but not before he'd had the best view and feel *ever* of
her boobs. They were for real! He was getting a hard
on just thinking about it. But once again for the
second night in a row, they laughed until tears came.
The more they tried to untangle, the more complicated it became. There were her boobs rubbing
against his chest and their heads together working at
some stupid little chain that went from one button
to the other. He could still hear her comment, when
they finally stopped laughing, and she stood up. "I'm
throwing this ridiculous blouse away and never wearing it again." (They'd had to break one of the little
chains, anyway.)

She left immediately and marched into her bedroom. When she returned, she had put on a sweater,
which didn't help his problem. At her appearance,
he announced that he was leaving stating that her
apartment caused him too many problems. In fact,
they'd both agreed. With the sofa springs Friday
night and the blouse tangle Saturday night, it was a

good thing he was leaving Sunday morning. If not they'd probably have to call out the fire department.

Once again he smiled at the memory. He was coming to the half-way point in his trip and decided to stop and eat. Furthermore, his thoughts kept going back to Penny and this wasn't like him at all. He wanted to concentrate on seeing his son.

The phone was ringing as she was opening her door. She hurried over and picked it up while stepping out of her shoes.

"Hello." (out of breath)

"Penny? Did I get you out of the tub,"

"Daisy Manning. God, it's good to hear your voice. No, I just got in the door from church."

"Oh sure. But it has been too long since we've visited, and having just re-read your last letter, I wasn't sure if you were still there."

"One more week. Gosh, Daze, you couldn't have called at a better time. How are my favorite godchildren and favorite ineligible?"

"We're all great, but how about you."

"I'm fine. Maybe just a little lonely, but I've got so much to do before I leave here that will pass quickly."

"I just knew there was some reason that I decided to call you today. What's this lonely bit? You've always been the one to lift my spirits."

(Hesitation)

"Well, I've had a visitor for the past four days, and he left this morning."

"Don't tell me—Lover Boy popped in on you

again, and for four whole days. You're probably just weak from combat. Where's he off to now?"

"Visiting his parents and his son in Illinois. He'll probably be coming back." (Combat! She laughed to herself remembering the button fiasco last night)

"What does that mean?"

"He expects to work here in Washington. He wants to get into television either behind the camera or in front. He had some interviews while he was here."

"God he moves in and you move out. Of course, I should have known."

"What does that mean?"

"You know how I feel about you and Sam. He's in love with you (ever since college, she thought) and too stubborn or stupid, I'm not sure which, to put that ring on your finger. And you're too proud to tell that jerk you feel the same way."

Penny laughed. "See I feel better already 'cause Daisy you're so entertaining."

"Just hope you're a good listener. How's the engineer?"

"That's complicated, too."

"Oh?"

"Yeah. You know we've been seeing each other for about six months and just enjoying a real pleasant relationship, and now would you believe he thinks he's in love with me."

"Oh God, and sometimes I think raising two kids and trying to keep my husband happy is a chore. So, you'll let him down gently. Right?" (because you're in love with Sam Boyer)

"Oh Daisy, it's rough. I am definitely not getting involved again, not ever."

"I've heard that before. You won't be in Lancaster one month until you'll be dating, and if Sam does get the job in Washington, I have an idea who you'll be seeing."

"Daisy, let's not waste your money talking such foolishness. If I can get some time off this summer could I come swim in your ocean?" (Just thinking of Virginia Beach, made her yearn for summer.)

"Oh, we'd love to have you. Its been almost a year. Just give me a call. How's your family? You'll be closer to home now, won't you."

"They ask about you every time I visit and yes I'll be a little closer and they're fine."

"Daze someone's at the door. Listen I'll send my new address and phone number just as soon as I get settled. Thanks again for calling and give my love to Al and the kids."

"Take care."

"I will. Bye."

"Coming." She pulled off her other earring and stuck them in her pocket, as she pulled open the door.

"You Miss Nagel?" She nodded. A little man who might have been in his forties and needed a shave, handed her a small package. "This is for you."

"Thank you." He turned and left.

When she took it from the bag, she realized that it was wrapped beautifully. She couldn't believe all the excitement since she'd gotten in the door from church.

First the call from Daisy, her dearest friend from

college days, and now a gift. There was a note inside, and under that a lovely little gold heart-shaped pin. It was just beautiful, and she could tell, quite expensive. The second she flipped the paper open, she recognized the handwriting. After all, they'd been corresponding for years. There was no salutation, just—"Thanks for a memorable visit. Here's my heart. Don't lose it." S.

Oh God, did he have to do this. She sat down on the sofa (the safe end) and lifted the pin from the bed of cotton. It was exquisite! Then she read the note again. Damn him! Then the tears came. For two cents, she'd send the darn pin back. And that "here's my heart" crap was downright sickening. Well, she wouldn't wear it! She got up went down the hall to her bedroom and put it away out of sight. Then she changed her clothes and started packing. When the phone rang again, it was Jason. She had thought today was going to be boring, and quiet after Sam's departure, but it was turning out to be rather traumatic. Now Jason wanted to come over. After her date with him Thursday night, when he'd gotten quite serious—she just didn't know what to expect. He was such a nice person and they enjoyed each other so much—in a quiet kind of way. In fact, she just wasn't sure about her feelings for him at all. And then she thought of Sam and what Daisy had said. She almost felt like a teen-ager again. She was so thoroughly confused.

"Still there."

"Yes, I'll be working 'cause I do need to get this packing finished."

"I promise. I'll help you pack."

"All right. Would you please pick up a loaf of bread from the deli? I'll fix tuna sandwiches."

"Good. See you shortly." She felt better already and went to the kitchen to make the tuna fish salad.

Al looked over at his wife as she hung up the phone. "I take it from your end of the conversation that Penny's heard from the roving reporter again."

Daisy looked very forlorn. "Come here and tell Papa all about it." He patted a space beside him on the sofa.

"Do you really want me to unload on you? After all, you listen to complaints all week."

"Penny's our friend and we're both interested in her welfare. Sure I want to hear."

"Honestly Al sometimes I could just kill that Sam Boyer. If he's not going to marry her, why doesn't he just leave her alone."

"Now wait a minute, honey, she doesn't have to see him."

"I know, but she's in love with him. And he's such a damn jackass. He's in love with her, too."

"You're sure? When we knew we loved each other, I asked you to marry me and you said 'yes'. Actually it's quite simple."

"Oh Al. I know that's the way it should be and usually is, but here we have two intelligent people playing a game and they're not getting any younger."

"What we have is a guy with an ego a mile wide and a mile high coupled with a bitterness toward marriage and a very attractive woman with high morals who expects him to ask her father for her hand in marriage, and in the meantime they're both miserable."

"Honey, I know why you're such a good lawyer, but now explain to me how we can help my dear, dear friend find our kind of happiness. Al, she'd make such a good mother, not to mention a great wife."

"She'll just have to get pregnant. That's why he married before."

"Oh, you—you're a big help. No way is that ever going to happen." She hit him with a pillow.

"I was kidding. I really don't think there's much we can do. However, I hope they come to their senses before she marries some other guy. She may decide to stop turning these men down, and opt for a husband and children—'cause you're right. She'd be terrific in both roles."

"I don't think she'd ever do that. The crazy part is that I think they've been in love since college."

"How's that?"

"Well, she met him through a minor staff position on the newspaper, and of course, since we were roommates, I knew she was impressed. So impressed, that by the end of the semester she'd decided that she would be a journalism major. It's crazy, really, she never actually dated him, but they worked very closely together. And she always made it a point to let any and all know that they were just friends and associates. I can't deny that Sam probably could have had his choice of girls, and did date the 'cream of the crop'; on occasion. But on a smaller scale at some inconsequential gatherings, he would escort some very questionable girls. Girls that were heavily made up and well endowed with low necklines. I must admit that there were times I pitied these floozies, but who made friends with them—Penny Nagel. Even though everyone knew why Sam dragged these oddballs along with him. Regardless who Penny was with, it was not unusual to see her sitting and talking with Sam's girl when he'd walk off and leave her alone. But when he attended a Class A function, he was sure to have a registered socialite on his arm. When this happened, one could still count on Sam saving at least one dance for Penny. Then when he graduated from college, he continued the correspondence and has never lost contact in all these years. Doesn't that strike you as peculiar?"

"Honey, look at the time, we've got to pick up the kids." Al and Daisy had two children, ages 7 and 10, Andrew and Peter. For the most part, theirs was a happy family. They wanted this same happiness for their friend, Penny. But for all their discussion, there were few options, and as they drove toward the skating rink, they both seemed to come to the same conclusion.

"You know Al, there really isn't much we can do for Penny, except pray."

"You're right Daze, and knowing Penny I'm sure she's already tapped that source."

"You're right. That is if she'll even admit to herself that he is the guy she wants." (Daisy had lived with Penny for four years and she knew. No way would that girl sacrifice her principles for a roll in the hay— even with Sam Boyer.)

*　　*　　*

He had just finished reading two chapters of the manuscript Penny had given him. He lit another cigarette, took another sip of his coffee that he'd brought back to his motel room, and rubbed his forehead. There were a few rough edges as far as presentation, but geez it was interesting. It wasn't easy to keep remembering that Penny had written this account of her parents' lives.

He'd called when he arrived earlier to make sure that Cal would be available for a visit and it seemed that everything was go. If he figured right, he'd pull in there tomorrow at around noon. Cal would be home from school in a few hours later and it would give Sam some time alone with Connie before the boy arrived home.

But damn here he was again lost in Penny's thoughts from reading her book. He decided to put the manuscript away for the night and plan on his visit. There was no plan, really. What does one do with a seven-year old boy when neither one knows the other. There was no way he could know what the boy would want to do. Well, he'd just have to wait and let the situation unfold. God, he thought, what a way to be a Dad. As he stared out at the neon lights above a restaurant across the street, the phone rang. He wouldn't be surprised if she canceled the visit.

"Hello."

"Sam, this is your mother. I called earlier, but you were out."

"Yes Mother, I was eating dinner."

"Well, you told me to let you know about any calls that came. A Mr. Ross Stanford called and wants you to call him at his home tonight. Do you want his number?"

"Sure, go ahead." Sam took down the info and thanked her for calling.

She asked him how his trip was going and if everything was all right. He assured her that he was fine and that he'd be seeing Cal tomorrow.

"Thanks again," and he hung up.

After retrieving his brief case from the car and going into his material regarding Stanford, he made the call.

Stanford explained the deal and seemed rather apologetic that the position didn't involve traveling, which was Boyer's style. Sam was almost certain that it would be a permanent set-up in Washington, writing and back-up in news delivery. (little did Stanford know that Sam was ready to sit in one place for awhile) Arrangements were made to meet again in two weeks when Sam would be expected to make a decision regarding a contract. He spent the next half hour studying all his material on the Stanford deal and was pleased.

He undressed and got into bed, pulling out Penny's manuscript once more, but had no sooner begun on the third chapter when the phone rang again.

"Hello."

"Sam, Hal Conner here. Hope I didn't interrupt anything important."

Sam laughed. "Don't I wish. What's on your mind?"

"Been thinking about your visit last week when you told me that you had lined up some interviews.

Had you given any thought to doing some overseas work for the State Department?"

"No, not really. Would you give me a thumb-nail sketch."

"Sure." Hal went into much more detail than Sam had in mind, but he listened patiently. They agreed to meet again when Sam arrived back in Washington. "Say, by the way, we liked Penny. It looked pretty serious. Is she the reason your checking on a position here?"

"Hardly, she's leaving. In fact, she'll be gone by the time I get back. She's not a big city girl."

"Sorry to hear that. You two seemed to hit it off real well."

"The roll of the dice, Hal. You know me, I never was very lucky with women. I arrive and she leaves."

Surprise! Yeah the call from Hal was quite a surprise. And again that word, overseas, nagged his thoughts even though he'd decided to stay put for awhile. The evening's events caused some anxiety, but after dousing another cigarette, he decided to call it a night. Tomorrow he'd visit with his son. The last thing he remembered before closing his eyes was Penny's reaction to "his heart." (as though he didn't know—in two words, hoppin mad)

In less than three days, he knew he'd lost him. Not once had the boy called him Dad. All conversation was monopolized with "yes and no sir." Furthermore, they didn't have much to say to each other. The afternoons, Thursday and Friday, that they had together when Cal came in from school were spent in awkward conversation. Connie was expecting a baby with her new husband, and there were questions in that regard. Did he like his stepfather? Would he like a baby sister or brother?

Information regarding Grandpa and Grandma took up much of the chit-chat, but Saturday when Sam took him to the Chicago Cubs game—they really enjoyed each other with all baseball talk and nothing else. (Thank the Lord for baseball, Sam thought)

Connie and her husband wanted to legally adopt —Sam said no. He saw the old Colonel, who was still directing from the trenches, and as domineering as ever. Happy in the knowledge that he'd found a son-in-law he could jerk around. The two of them had opened a retail TV/Communication Center with the old man running the show. He mentioned Sam's book and requested an autographed copy upon publication.

Bruce, husband number two, came across as a handsome devil, devoted to Connie and Cal, and thrilled to be a part of her family's empire. Sam made a decision to leave on Sunday. He had a gut feeling, even though Connie implied that the boy could come for a visit in the summer, that Cal would never really be *his* son and that this could possibly be his last visit. (There would probably be occasional visits in the summer, but not as intimate father/son.)

That part of his life had passed him by and he must learn to accept what couldn't be changed. Right before he left, he did make a request of Connie that she write his parents at specific times with news of their grandson, and maybe send them a picture on occasion. (He did make a promise to himself that he would take the boy to visit them this summer.) It certainly wasn't fair to the grandparents to lose a grandson so completely.

That night from his motel room, he finished Penny's book and he decided to call her. But after three tries when there was no answer, he gave up. He called Barney in St. Louis. They went back to WWII. Of any man that he'd ever become good friends with, he guessed Barney was more like him than any other. Barney had started a cargo plane service after his discharge, and it turned out to be a lucrative business. They would be spending a couple of days together before he headed back to D.C.

He was exhausted and thought he'd go right off, but instead he kept thinking about Penny's book. It was around 2 a.m. when he got up from a restless slumber, lit a cigarette, and stared out the window— seeing a neon sign The Checkers Restaurant—that he remembered the night she had talked him into playing checkers.

"It's your move."

"No, it isn't. I just moved."

"Sam that was two moves ago and if you don't go now, I'm going to hop you all over the place."

"Okay." He sat back and folded his arms across his chest.

"I'll not make another move. Go ahead and follow through with your threat." He laughed. Checkers didn't excite him very much.

No it was just too late, or early, he thought, as he put down the phone. He crushed his cigarette butt in the ash tray and went back to bed.

* * *

She was worn out, but knew she was finally ready for the movers who would be arriving in the morning. Furthermore, she wasn't happy with herself since she had told Jason that their association would have to remain strictly friendship. With the miles now separating the two, it didn't seem likely that she would hear from him again. Her memories of D.C. would be left behind—whether that was good or bad, only time would tell.

Monday night, Barney and Sam were feeling no pain during an evening of partying at the local pub when Sam decided to call Penny. However, the operator informed him that the phone had been disconnected. "I told you Barn our love life appears to be mired in the mud. My little woman has abandoned me." It was early in the morning when they staggered out to a cab singing, "I want a girl just like the girl that married dear old Dad."

Sam started back to Washington with a splitting headache, but anxious to get to work. He was ready!

"Miss Nagel's phone."

"Could I speak to Miss Nagel?

"Hold on please."

"Penny Nagel. Can I help you?"

"Oh baby can you ever."

It was slightly over a month, and here he was again. Ignoring his remark, she answered, "Sam—how you doing?"

"I'm running the government for Ike, but taking a break from my busy schedule to check on you."

"I'm honored. When's your next press conference. I'll try to be present."

"Is that a promise?"

"Yes. It has been sometime since we've had a gab session.

She wanted to hear of his visit with his ex-wife and son, and also his new job.

"You're serious aren't you."

"Never more."

"Do you have every other week-end free?"

"Yes. Mine happens to be the week-end coming up."

"Well, I've got my own place which I'd like you to see and help me furnish. I'm not too far from your former address."

"Good then I won't have too much trouble locating the street."

"What time can I expect you?"

"Around 10, all right?"

"How's it going at the New Era? Ten's fine."

"Great, and I want to hear all about your new job—when you're not assisting Ike. Ha Ha"

"See you Saturday. Don't lose the address and you've got my home phone number. And Ike's."

"Bullseye! Geez, I almost forgot. Can I get a room at your favorite motel?"

"No."

"Why?"

"No rooms to unescorted ladies."

"Come on Boyer. I know I'm small town, but not that small."

"Well, you can't blame a guy for trying. God, this is really comical. The last time we met here—I was at the motel. I'd say it's time we get our act together."

"That's debatable. Gotta go, Sam—see ya."

"Bye."

He looked around at his apartment. It really did need some furniture. He had a bed, an alarm clock, small radio, and two chairs from his card table set of four. Of course, his living room, dining room, and kitchen area was really sparse. He'd even settle for her broken down sofa now. Not a damn piece of furniture conducive for necking. Well, there was the bed. But knowing Penny, he could forget that. Oh well, he'd get her a really nice motel room and they could spend their time there. He was whistling as he walked into his office a short time later. Mrs. Grantham, his secretary, looked up from her desk.

"Someone's in a good mood."

She was a little older than what he would have liked, but she certainly was efficient and very outgoing. He supposed that he could have chosen another person but he was well satisfied after the first week.

"Sometimes a phone call effects me that way. Would you take a few minutes and get me a motel reservation for Saturday night in the vicinity of my address. First class," he added.

"Of course Sam." (He'd insisted on the first name for him)

Amy Grantham liked her new boss. He was pleasant and easy to please, and S-E-X-Y. Boy! If she were only 20 years younger. This room must be for the woman who left the Post several months ago. He'd mentioned her once or twice. He kept no pictures on his desk nor anywhere in his office. Sort of a loner, but with the kind of life he led—this didn't surprise her.

She'd seen his resume and knew that he was divorced and had one son. However, there had never been any mention of either one. He frequently made caustic remarks and didn't laugh too often, but she wasn't convinced that he was unhappy. Just not fulfilled.

"Grantham," he called out to her. Another habit from his background, she imagined, using her last name only. She didn't mind because she had grown very fond of Sam Boyer in the last month.

"Coming," and she hurried in with her short hand tablet.

CHAPTER VI

PENNY HAD a little car trouble right outside of Baltimore, but Sophie perked up after filling her tank with gas and adding a little oil. As she drove along, she was thinking of the heart pin which he hadn't mentioned and she didn't intend to, either. Darn, she was anxious to see him, and it hadn't been that long. She thought of Daisy's words again, "The only one you'll be dating will be Sam Boyer."

When she pulled into the parking lot of the luxurious high-rise apartment building, she noticed Sam immediately. He was talking to another man next to his car. He saw her at the same time and came right over.

After helping her out and giving her a big bear hug, she could detect his anxiety, as he said, "God, Penny I was getting concerned. You did say 10?" (He looked at his watch.)

"Sorry, not deliberate. Sophie and I had a slight disagreement right outside of Baltimore, but from there on she cooperated."

As he took her arm and led her toward the entrance, "Well I think she needs a transplant."

She explained to him what happened as they went up on the elevator and he planned to check the car over before she returned to Lancaster.

It was a beautiful day, and although Penny had on a new cotton sun dress with a little jacket, she felt rather wilted. Little beads of perspiration had formed around her lips and damp strands of hair fell alongside her face. But Sam didn't seem to mind.

Once the door had closed, he took her into his arms and his lips found hers. He had on a summer shirt which was partially unbuttoned and she could see a few dark hairs on his chest. As always he created feelings in her which were so hard to control. She loved the taste of him and now the hair on his chest. Geez, she just hoped he couldn't guess how much.

When he finally let her go, he said, "Wow, you taste good—good enough to eat." And with his lips just inches away, she said softly, "I need to wash my face and hands before we do too much kissing. I'm all perspired." Furthermore, it had been awhile, and they both needed to cool off.

Reluctantly he let her go. "Come on I'll show you the bathroom."

For the first time, she looked around. "Sam you don't have any furniture!"

"You noticed."

She laughed. "I'll say one thing. You don't do too much entertaining in this apartment."

"I've got a bed."

"Why am I not surprised."

She'd barely gotten into the bathroom and seated on the toilet when he knocked on the door.

"Yes."

"I just remembered. There's towels and wash cloths in that right drawer—and they're clean."

"Okay. I'll find them. Thanks."

Geez, she thought, he always had to wait until she got in the bathroom to start a conversation.

After she checked into her motel, which was super deluxe, they had lunch and then went shopping for furniture.

Penny couldn't remember when she had ever enjoyed herself so much. Sam seemed to go along with all her choices. Oh, maybe once or twice he expressed an opinion, but by and large—he left it up to her. That night when she saw his bedroom before they went out to dinner, she felt a pang of sadness. There were two large trunks pushed up against the wall which probably contained all his worldly possessions. He had been knocking around for years on his own and this was probably the first time he had a home since his brief encounter with marriage. She wondered if he missed it and couldn't be sure.

He described his writing assignment and impressed her with his commitments, but she could sense just slightly that itch to be on the move. He was such an enigma—this guy.

They sat in her motel room on the comfy chairs with their feet propped up on the bed until midnight. He brought a bottle of wine and some beer. They talked about everything. How his ex-wife was pregnant, and he felt that he'd lost his son; his visit with Barney Edwards (and his marital problems); his job; and his plans to take Cal to visit his parents in July.

He liked her story and wanted to keep the manuscript. Since she had the original, of course, she didn't mind. His plaudits regarding her writing were quite flattering and he hoped that sometime he could meet her parents. In fact, he was fascinated by the entire Nagel clan. He knew that his family had never experienced such closeness. He expressed this to Penny.

"You could be wrong Sam. Not everyone can express their feelings outwardly, but feel great love and respect in their hearts."

"I like the outward expression myself," and he pulled her onto his lap.

She had taken off her dinner dress and put on her dressing gown which had a zipper in front up to her neck—so no buttons could catch, and of course, had kicked off her shoes.

"I had a great time today Sam. I loved choosing your furniture. I hope you remember how I suggested you place each piece."

"Geez, how can I forget. You had me sketch the entire apartment on back of my cleaning bill."

"Knowing you—that'll be lost by tomorrow night."

"Sam, I'll be visiting my old church tomorrow morning. I hope you don't mind."

"Mind? Why should I? What do you think I am—an atheist? I'll go along—if you'd like."

"You will!" Her arms flew around his neck, and she kissed him on the cheek.

"Pen take it easy," and he carefully moved her over slightly on his lap. "We got a snarl down here," and he grimaced as his hand went under her bottom to touch his genitals.

"Oh Sam. I'm sorry. Should I move?"

"No babe—just sit still and try to control your emotions. (His hands moved over her derriere.) Now back to tomorrow. I can't go to church on an empty stomach."

"Well I can't think about breakfast now if you insist on massaging my rump."

"I thought you'd like that," he said laughing.

"You're so darn smart, Sam Boyer. I like to eat breakfast, too."

"Hell, if I were really smart, I'd be out of here right now. Where will we eat?"

"Thanks a heap! I'll pick up some Danish on the way over to your apartment and I noticed you have some eggs and coffee in your kitchen."

"Okay with me. Now I better get out of here 'cause you're yawning and I'm getting horny."

She slipped off his lap and knew what he meant.

He picked up his coat, and once again had to be reminded of his shoes.

"Penny we did have fun today. I'm glad you came to visit. You're my first guest, and I won't lose my cleaning bill."

"Good. Once you furnish those fancy digs, you'll be entertaining all the time."

"Hardly. I don't know how."

"That's debatable," she answered. (but somehow she knew he was probably telling the truth)

"Next time we see each other, it will be at your place anyway. I'm looking forward to seeing your home and I don't trust Sophie."

"Bullseye."

He now had on his shoes, stood up, and took her into his arms.

"Goodnight babe. I am rather sleepy. I couldn't sleep last night thinking about your visit." He gave her a "slider" kiss, and was gone. His last words were "Make sure you lock the door and don't open it."

Sometime later, she turned on her radio, low volume, so as not to disturb other guests, when her phone rang.

"Penny, you asleep."

"No Sam, I'm listening to *The Nearness of You* on the radio."

"Damn, I thought I was sleepy when I left, now I'm wide awake. The nearness of you. What's it do to you?"

"I'll never tell."

"God this place is lonely. We've known each other a long time; you can tell me."

"What? Now they're playing *One for the Road.*"

"You can change the subject as fast as the station changes the music. What station is it?" When she told him—he tuned his radio on to the same music.

"Did you find it?"

"Yes, I found one for the road, and it's in my hand."

"I'm glad you waited until you arrived home."

"Babe I never imbibe to the extreme when I know I'm driving." (Then, as an added afterthought) "Did you receive a package before you left Alexandria?"

"A package?"

"Well, sort of a little package."

"Why?"

"Damn! Penny you did receive the heart pin I sent, didn't you?"

She laughed. "Was that from you? It was just signed 'S' and I wasn't sure. I did date a Steve one time."

"You didn't like it? Steve who?"

"Oh, I liked the pin. The note was rather gushy, though."

"I thought it was quite good. In fact, I thought it was very good."

"You would."

"I haven't seen you wear it."

"I might lose it."

"No you won't. You wouldn't dare."

"Geez, what an ego. Furthermore, you can't be sure that I'm not wearing it."

"Good Lord, what'd you do—pin it on your panties."

Penny laughed. "You're falling asleep. You're talking crazy—you know that. I have worn it. I just didn't have it on tonight. The pin is lovely. Thank you."

"Are you ticked off because of the note? And I'm not asleep. I was feeling romantic at the time. That's not egotistical."

"All right. I'll take your word, but you don't seem

like the romantic type, friend." She was becoming exasperated with his game.

"You don't know what I'm feeling inside."

"Do you?"

"Yes—no. Hell, Penny. I am going to sleep or I shouldn't have had another beer before climbing into bed. (His voice slurred into a mumble)

"See you at breakfast. Good night Sam."

"Sweet dreams."

"Yeah, sure"—she said to herself and hung up.

He stood there in only his shorts as he slowly opened the door, rubbing his eyes and half asleep, said, "I don't want any."

Penny had never seen Sam so close to being naked and it took all her will power to act unruffled by the line of hair running down his chest and beneath his shorts. He had the body of a man who looked as though he never guzzled beer or smoked a cigarette. God! She never dreamed he looked so masculine and desirable under that crooked tie and often wilted collar, but she hoped her response came across very matter-of-factly, "I'm not selling. But if you'll open the door and let me in, I will prepare your breakfast."

He was very observing and even in his drowsy state she knew he was aware of her sensitivity to his *almost* nakedness. She was equally certain that the women in his life would not be affected by any physical change simply because they were not 33-year-old virgins. His lady friends had "been around the barn" a few times, whereas she hadn't even gained access to the door.

As he rubbed his eyes again, he said, "Geez, Penny

what time did you get up," and he looked at his watch.

"I got up in time," as she walked to his kitchen, "to make you breakfast and get to church by eleven."

He stood there looking at her as she began preparations for making their breakfast. She was dressed impeccably in a blue suit that matched her eyes, and moved gracefully from the stove, to the fridge, and then to the table.

"I'm sorry. On Sundays, I usually sleep in, but don't worry I'll be ready. I'm going to take my shower and get dressed. Okay."

"Fine." She couldn't look at him, but kept busy.

"I do have a shower in the master bedroom, so if you need the bathroom, feel free."

"Thanks." She was glad when he moved away and toward his bedroom.

A few minutes later the phone rang. When he didn't answer her call, she decided to get it.

"Hello."

"Hello. Is Sam there?"

"Yes, but he's in the shower. Could I take a message or have him return your call?"

"Sure. Just tell him to call Amy. He's got the number. It's important."

"Will do."

She went down toward his room again and called once more. The shower had been turned off. It was silly to resent Amy's call. She knew Sam was sexually active. But she did! "Sam, are you presentable," she called.

"Yeah babe. I'm in here shaving."

She looked toward the open door. He now had a

towel wrapped around his middle. His hair was combed and there were traces of shaving cream smeared on his face. This time she thought he looked kind of cute.

"Sam your phone rang while you were in the shower, so I answered."

"And . . ."(as he moved the razor down his jaw)

"It was Amy and she wants you to call her. She said it was important."

"Thanks. I didn't hear the phone."

She wished he would have. She already didn't like Amy, whoever she was. Penny began to re-evaluate her friendship with Sam. Her dilemma was maintaining a friendship for a guy who was actually more than a friend—to her, anyway. It hurt!

She had the eggs already to scramble, but decided to wait until he was dressed, and finished with his phone call.

He walked into the kitchen—all dressed except for his tie. His collar was unbuttoned at the neck. He came over, turned her around and pulled her to him. "Good morning Penny," and his lips found hers and held. Geez, he smelled so good and was so smooth shaven and clean.

The aroma of coffee filled the air, a paper plate with delicious pastries was centered on the card table, and there were paper cups filled with fresh orange juice. He observed all the amenities as he loosened his hold slightly. "I do appreciate this lovely breakfast. It was very kind of you to come here and prepare this feast."

As she turned slightly, and said, "I must do the eggs."

"Wait," and he pulled her back, "I also want to thank you for taking Amy's message. She's my secretary, and she's 60, if she's a day."

She looked into his eyes, and said rather defensively, "Explanations aren't necessary." (However, she felt relieved)

"I know that Penny. Just thought you'd like to know." (He laughed.) "Actually, I was hoping you might be jealous." His entire face was in a full smile from his laughing blue eyes to his wide spread mouth showing every perfect white incisor.

Her suit coat was draped over the folding chair and she had tied a towel around her waist. This time she did pull away.

"God, you've got such an ego, Boyer, with your sashaying around here like Tarzan ever since I arrived and now I should be feint of heart because of one damn phone call."

Now he really gave out with a hearty laugh, as she poured the eggs into his one frying pan. She knew her face was flushed. He sure could get under her skin.

"You really are jealous." He came over to the stove, put his arms around her waist and kissed her neck under her hair.

Softly he said, as he continued to hold her, "My favorite journalist and little Susie Homemaker, too."

"The eggs are ready."

"And Tarzan's hungry."

She started to laugh then, and they regained their amiable relationship. They both ate heartily, and when she left the table to get the coffee pot, he noticed the lapel of her jacket.

"You have my heart."

"I've what?"

"On your lapel."

"It's exquisite." (He beamed.)

"So was that breakfast."

Fifteen minutes later they left for church. Sam looked so neat and most attractive as he accompanied her to a pew down in the sanctuary of St. John's Lutheran Church. As they sang *Holy, Holy, Holy,* she noticed that he sang a fair baritone. Since his speaking voice was impressive, it shouldn't have surprised her.

By 2 p.m. she was on her way back to Lancaster. He had checked her car the day before and felt that she should have no problems but made her promise to call him if she did. He gave her his office phone number, since he was going there when she left. They were doing a thing on Senator Joseph McCarthy.

"Thanks for—"

"I enjoyed my—"

They both spoke at the same time.

"You first."

"I enjoyed my weekend."

"I enjoyed having you."

He gave her a "slider" kiss, and she was on her way. As she neared Lancaster, she remembered his questions concerning Jason at the restaurant last night.

"What was his reaction when you told him that he'd have to settle for friendship?"

"You don't want to know."

"Why?"

"You might get ideas and I enjoy our friendship."

"Let me guess. He wanted more and wasn't about to take on a long distance courtship without the pot of gold at the end of the rainbow."

"You're so darn smart Boyer. That's not exactly his words, but the message was similar. He decided there was someone else, I might add."

"He was right, too."

"No."

"There's me."

"Oh God, there's always you. He was talking a 'serious' someone else."

Sam was very quiet for awhile. But when they danced and he held her close, she remembered his words, *every one*, and probably would never forget them, when he softly said in her ear, "I *am* that someone else and we both know it."

Upon pondering Sam's remark once again, Penny realized their so-called friendship was gradually, but most surely developing into more. In past years, their visits had been a year or years apart. Oh they'd written more, but now the close proximity of their environs allowed for the phone to replace the letters and actual visits becoming much more frequent.

She also gleaned from what Sam said that his past marriage was definitely a chapter closed with his ex-wife pregnant to husband number two. Also, the fervor for his son, Cal, had diminished greatly. He had stated as a point of fact which must be accepted that the boy was lost to him as a Daddy.

Actually, Daisy had summed up the situation pretty well, and now the next move was up to Penny.

Or was it? She had no guarantee that Sam was not seeing other women, although he implied as much when he assured her that Amy was his 60-year old secretary. And she, Penny, had practically assured him that she was not seeing anyone. So, she was back at square one with their association becoming an even greater dilemma than at any time during the many years of their acquaintance. Penny had always considered herself a realist—not one to fantasize, so why change now. Fact—she loved Sam Boyer. Fact— he liked her. If God in his infinitesimal wisdom felt the two should be together—it would happen. If not, and Sam left the country on another mission or found another Connie, then she would have to ac- cept that, too. In the meantime, she would continue to lead a busy life at the newspaper, at church, and with her family. She knew it would not be easy. But she grew up knowing that life is not always fair, nor easy; and when it is the value diminishes. Geez, she didn't even have a picture of Sam. (only the one on the jacket of his WWII book) Whoopee!

Her desk was piled high and she was glad. For the next two weeks she was really "snowed under." When she found time to prop up her feet, having finally whipped her home into shape (she'd gotten the spring tied down in her sofa, and it didn't look bad), she called Sam.

After letting it ring about eight times, she hung up. She had arrived home late after serving as guest speaker at a B & P Woman's Club in Lancaster. Since she was working on a feature story for the paper *Life In A Trailer Park*, she crawled into bed to read some research she'd accumulated.

Talk about ESP—her phone rang about 30 minutes later.

"Hello."

"Hi, Sam here."

"Would you believe that I called you a little while ago. What's up?"

"I'll give you two guesses."

"I won't even make one, so shoot."

"Damn you make it rough for me to carry on a decent conversation."

"Bullseye. I haven't seen you for a month and you pick up right where you left off. No 'how are you' or 'miss me'."

"Okay, sorry. How are you? Did you miss me?"

"Busy and yes, Okay." She laughed.

"Too busy for a visit from your favorite journalist."

"Never."

"When's a good time?"

"Next weekend."

"Bad for me."

"You asked."

"This weekend is out?"

"Yes."

"Yes, what."

"Yes, it's out."

"Let me see if I can do some juggling. You know I'm planning a visit for Cal with the Boyer grandparents later on this month, so I'll be taking some time off then."

"I know, and I don't want our time together to jeopardize that visit in any way."

"I'll call you when I see what can be arranged for next weekend. You said a little while ago? I must have been in the damn shower. I can't hear a thing in there."

"I know."

"You can't either. We'll just have to stop taking showers. Unless . . . No that's out of the question. Are you in bed?"

"Yes. Just barely—I'm reading. How about you?"

"Lying here happy as a clam as I survey my new interior decor."

"Oh Sam! How does everything look? Are you satisfied?"

"It looks great and I'm more than satisfied. I'm ecstatic. At last I'm ready to entertain. I think I'll throw a party. Would you be my hostess?"

"There would be a small fee, but sure. You're serious, aren't you?"

"Sure. Let's plan it, if I can manage next weekend, and if I can manage your fee."

"You can."

"You'd be amazed at all the fetes I can perform, if you'd just let me."

She laughed. "You made a believer out of me a long time ago. I know! I know! In spite of that, you're still my best friend."

"God, talk about a back handed compliment. Don't do me any favors, Nagel," he teased.

"C'mon Sam, this is Penny. No routines, please. We both know what kind of fetes you're referring to."

"Geez, how did I ever get roped into an association with such a 'Miss Know-it-all'."

"You couldn't help yourself."

"You got that right—I still can't. Are you wearing your night shirt?"

"No, I'm in the buff."

"If that's a come-on, it's working. But you're kidding."

"You're right. I'm in my night shirt."

"How about you?"

"Not a damn thing."

"Why?"

"None of your business."

He probably didn't have any clean shorts, or only had one pair and wanted to save them for tomorrow. His clothes supply wasn't the greatest.

"Sorry. I didn't mean to pry. Little edgy, aren't you?"

"Oh babe, I didn't mean to sound off at you, but that damn hamper we bought fills up too fast and I just haven't had time to take my laundry to that Chinese guy you referred. I promise I will tomorrow. I'm just not used to this white collar and tie job everyday." (plus clean shorts, he thought)

"When you come to Lancaster I hope you'll agree to go shopping *for you*. I had three brothers so I'm pretty good at picking out men's clothes."

"You're on. I just dread buying clothes."

"You'd better be able to manage next weekend 'cause we have so much to do."

"Damn. I'll be there. If any kind of emergency comes up—I'll call."

"Are you sure?"

"I'm sure. Saturday around 10, Okay."

"Bye Sam."

"Sweet dreams Penny."

How could she ever imagine her life without Sam Boyer! She laughed to herself as she remembered his comment about the hamper. She'd gotten him the largest size they had.

That was the end of her research for the night. Now just so he could make it next weekend.

CHAPTER VII

Sᴀᴍ ʜᴀᴅ arrived late, after calling, and then had appeared with a new short haircut. He looked so different. Penny was surprised that he no longer had that slicked down, well-combed look. If the truth be known, this new short haircut was much more akin to his personality and she decided she liked it.

The hearings in Washington were keeping him "nailed down," as he stated. She even felt guilty in expecting him to make the trip this weekend. And of course he did seem preoccupied. Buying his clothes at the two leading department stores, Hagers and Watt & Shand, was left almost completely up to her. However, she did manage to have him try on a suit, a pair of slacks, and a sport coat. He reneged at shoes —saying he had plenty.

It definitely did not start out as one of their more

pleasant visits. He grumbled about her house being stuck in a long row of look-alikes.

"Damn Penny, I felt so stupid parading around finding your number. But when he saw her interior decoration, he became somewhat subdued. Except for the sofa, which he felt should have been left in Alexandria.

They visited the markets which he enjoyed and took in some local sights. He was very impressed with the city and the paper. Consequently, by the time she cooked him supper (which she insisted on), he was in a much better mood. He dozed off on the sofa and when she finished in the kitchen, she slipped into the living room, stooped over and kissed him on the forehead. Suppressing her desire to run her fingers through the wiry, short hair was too much —so she did just that. He opened one eye, looked up at her and pulled her onto the sofa.

"You're asking for trouble Nagel, running your fingers through my hair."

"Well, no, just a friendly smooch or two." (Her eyes sparkled)

"You're sure we're safe on this trigger happy sofa?"

"Yes, but let's make sure."

He couldn't get enough of her, nor she of him.

No words were spoken. Just kissing, touching, and sounds of utter delight.

Finally he said, "The sofa passed the test, but I'm not doing too well."

"Oh Sam, I'm doing too well, but you're right. It's break time."

Gently, he moved her away. God, she looked sexy.

Her lips were slightly swollen and her soft, sweet scented hair was falling around his face.

"Penny, do you know there's some freckles on your nose?"

She pulled her head back. "Geez, I thought this mood was supposed to be romantic, and you're reminding me I have freckles."

"They're kind of cute. I never noticed them before."

"For your information, they only pop out in the summer."

"Well, babe for your information, if you don't let me up, I have something that will pop out." He began working his way off the sofa.

He stepped over his parcels, and headed for the kitchen.

"They're on the top shelf in the back." God, his comments had a way of bringing out the perspiration. Right now, she felt hotter than a chili pepper.

"I think I'll have one—I need to cool off."

He heard her call to him. Serves her right, he thought. He took a little longer than was necessary to open two bottles of beer. (Penny with a beer. He was tickled.)

As he returned to the living room, and handed one to her he said, with a mischievous grin, "That necking gets to you after awhile—doesn't it?"

As she took a gulp from the bottle, she said, "Well, it is kind of warm in here."

"Warm, hell, it's hotter than a smoking pistol and we both know it." He sat on the chair, pulled off his tie and unbuttoned his shirt.

Penny was still sitting on the sofa. Her face was

flushed with ringlets of perspiration lining her hairline. "You got that right, Boyer," and she began a fanning motion with her hand. She surveyed her appearance which was in disarray. Her skirt and blouse were twisted and her sandals had been kicked off and were in the middle of the floor.

Sam was smoking a cigarette, as he studied her. Inwardly he decided that he had never seen her so hot and bothered. She was flustered for sure. She looked down and tried to straighten her blouse and skirt as she crossed her bare, well-shaped legs. She had acquired a tan already which was very becoming. When she pulled out her handkerchief and began wiping her face, he laughed.

"What's so funny?"

"You."

"Why? It's the beer and because I look like some floozie."

"Sure, you're my floozie. C'mon admit it. You got the hots for me."

"Well, I do like your new haircut. I just didn't realize how much." She laughed. "Now when you parade around in those new duds, those chicks in D.C. won't let you rest."

"I know and it will be your fault. How'd you get that nice tan?" he asked, as he slipped on his loafers.

"Changing the subject on me, Lover Boy. I go swimming. You still want to go bowling?"

"Babe I really think *we'd better* go bowling."

He went back to his motel to shower and change, and then came back and picked her up. She and Sam enjoyed their evening with her friends from the church. He hadn't bowled for years, but then none of the group seemed to be expert rollers—so the camaraderie was a high for Sam and even though they were exhausted as they parted, he and Penny shared another great time together.

He begged off from church the next morning and she understood. Saturday had been a killer for him. They went out to Sunday dinner and Sam was fascinated by the Amish buggies they passed. Penny drove since she wanted him to see the Amish farms and beautiful Lancaster landscape. He was astounded at the beauty of the environment and there were no words to describe his feelings. Unusual for a writer! The dinner was also quite an experience. The food was delicious and so different from any he had ever eaten. As he finished a large serving of shoo fly pie, he made the remark that if he lived in the area, his new suit soon wouldn't fit.

Later they went to Long's Park, sat on a blanket in the shade of a large maple tree, and made plans for Sam's cocktail party. They tentatively set the date for the third Saturday in July. Sam would have his secretary, Amy Grantham, contact Penny and between them they would plan the beverage and hors d'oeuvre list, send out invitations, employ a caterer, and finalize the guest list. Together they made a tentative list of the guests. His publisher and agent, his three bosses, Hal Conner, Greg Thornhill, Ellen Scaratelli, plus Sam and herself. They decided with spouses/friends included the number would come to 18. They both agreed that was enough.

He was so grateful for her help and just hoped his first venture into entertaining would not be a flop. Penny assured him that if Amy was an efficient secretary, there was no way his party would not be a great success. They were all business on the blanket that afternoon in their knee-length shorts and tennis shoes. (for awhile that is)

They had stopped on their way and bought hamburgers, french fries, and cokes. After an hour of planning, Sam had had his fill and was ready for some horseplay. She remembered his short interest span the night she had talked him into playing gin rummy. He reluctantly agreed after she flatly refused to play strip poker. The game was fine for about 20 minutes, and then it exploded into a rout. He brazenly admitted that he had cheated. "Hell, Penny how else do you make this boring game exciting." The card game ended.

"Now don't forget to tell Amy to write me and you be sure and check your calendar when you get back. Okay?"

They were in their barefeet and lying on the blanket side by side. "Yes dear, I promise," he replied as if he learned the words by rote. He was bored with party talk and Penny knew it.

He was now playing footsies. As she looked down, he had wrapped his big foot around hers.

"Did you know your second toe is crooked?"

He held up his foot and moved his toes. "Damned if you're not right. Hold your foot up." She did and placed it aside his.

"Okay, so your feet are smaller and no crooked toes, but I have hair on mine and you don't."

"Aren't you glad I don't?" she said laughing.

"Yeah, I wouldn't want to see that dirty blond hair

on those pretty toes." He had begun pulling the ribbon from her pony tail.

"Sam will you be driving the whole way to Illinois and then back to Buffalo with Cal?"

"I guess so, why?" He was playing with the ribbon.

"Geez, that's an awful grind. Then after a few days, you drive him back to Illinois."

"I know, and I'm not looking forward to it, but I promised my parents a visit with Cal. Who knows, during our round trip, he may call me Dad, instead of sir."

"God for your sake, I hope so. It would certainly make the trip more enjoyable if you two could establish a rapport."

"Penny, don't be concerned. I've accepted my role in his life and I'm not expecting any pleasant surprises. However, on occasion I would like him to call me Dad. That's all."

"That little fellow doesn't realize how fortunate he is to have Sam Boyer as a father." She was very serious as she turned her head to face him.

He held her face between his hands and kissed her. "That was a very kind comment, and I know you meant it." He was tempted to say, I wish you were his mother. But of course that wasn't Sam's style. So he followed his statement with, "Babe this is most enjoyable, but 'til we get back and I get my parts moving—it will be nightfall."

"Oh I know." They both began putting on their shoes and socks. She folded the blanket and picked up her papers while he took their empty bags and bottles to the trash basket. Another visit about over, she thought, but for the first time ever, she did know for sure when the next one was—the third Saturday in July. That's progress! Upon leaving Sam, she never said call me or write, she left that up to him. But it was comforting to know that in about five weeks she would be seeing him again. And once again she thought of Daisy's remark, "Sam will be the only one you'll be dating."

When they walked into her house a half hour later, her phone was ringing.

"Hello."

"Hi Penny. Jim Krider, Sports, remember?"

"Sure, Jim, I know you and I enjoy your column." He was a real nice guy on the staff. She had chatted with him several times—a little shy, but pleasant. Not bad looking, either! However, she had given him no reason to expect any more.

He probably detected that she was out of breath when she answered the phone, and said, "Is this a bad time?"

"Well yes. Could you call back later?"

"Sure. Bye."

"Bye."

Sam had come up behind her and his arms went around her waist. "Aha," he said close to her ear, "sounds as though I'm getting competition—again."

She turned around and put her arms around his neck, as she said, "Would you mind?"

"Need you ask." His lips found hers and they kissed. When he finally released her, his blue eyes bore into hers, "Are you convinced? I could stay here all night if you're not sure."

"Yes."

"I can. Wow!" He pulled her to him again.

"You looney tunes. Yes, I'm convinced. You knew what I meant."

He backed away putting up both hands, palms out, "Let me down gently."

"I'm trying."

"That'll be the day." He laughed.

"Okay, wise guy. How about hitting that diner that I suggested earlier. It might be a trifle greasy, but you can't drive back to D.C. on an empty stomach."

"You're right. Must I change?"

"No, but those sexy legs could get you into a peck of trouble."

"With the truck drivers?"

"Sure. Who else?"

After that crack, she ran toward the stairs, and he was after her.

"Sam, I'm going to put slacks on."

"When you're out of the bathroom, call down."

"I'm out," she yelled, as she went into her bedroom and closed the door.

Fifteen minutes later, they walked the three blocks to the diner. Her neighbors, the real friendly ones, the Donleys, were on their front porch.

They probably were her parents' age and very suspicious of her when she first moved in—a young woman living alone. Penny grew up in a small town so she knew what they were thinking. But she straightened Mrs. Donley out the first time they talked and Mr. Donley was a dear. He made her promise to call on him if she had any problems. They were sitting on their front porch in quiet conversation as she and Sam came out the front door.

"Evening Penny. Certainly has been a beautiful day."

"You're so right." She looked at Sam and then at the Donleys, as she said, "Mr. & Mrs. Donley I'd like you to meet my friend, Sam Boyer."

Mr. Donley immediately stood up and moved over to the railing that separated the two porches, and throwing out his hand, said, "Pleased to meet you Mr. Boyer." They exchanged a hearty handshake and pleasant greetings. "It's a pleasure to meet you both," Sam said, including Mrs. Donley in the introduction.

"Any friend of Penny's is our friend. She has certainly been a good neighbor."

"That's good to hear Mr. Donley. She's been a great friend to me, also. We're going to try out the diner down the street. Would you two like to join us?" Sam responded.

"Oh thank you ever so much Mr. Boyer, but we've already eaten. Their food's not bad."

"Well, that's good to hear. Nice meeting you both."

"Same here. Goodnight."

"Goodnight." They both said together.

They walked down the steps and up the sidewalk. "How thick are those walls, Penny?"

"Why?"

"Just thinking about that motel last March in Alexandria." He was tickled.

Penny laughed, too. "I'm glad I had the spring fixed in the sofa."

"Oh God, me, too." They were oblivious to others

sitting on their front porches as they walked along the street laughing.

Within a week Penny heard from Amy Grantham. This was the beginning of a warm friendship between the two women. Also, within the same week, on Wednesday, Eva Nolt, another reporter came in carrying a florist box. "Penny, look what I have for you. They were left at the front desk." Eva was all smiles, and Penny was all thumbs. Once again, she looked at a dozen beautiful long-stemmed red roses. She pulled out the card. It read "Thanks for showing me Lancaster." S.

"Oh Penny they're beautiful."

In Eva's excitement, she didn't notice a tear, or two (maybe) as Penny read the card. Why, oh why Sam?

"I'll go find a vase or a jar, or something to put them in," and she hurried out of the office.

When Jim Krider came by the news room later that day, he also noticed the roses and he had his answer.

He had asked her Monday if she would consider going to the July 4th annual picnic with him. Although she would be attending, she planned on going with some of the ladies in her office. She thanked him.

"Fletch, how's about meeting at the Red Rose for lunch."

"Okay by me Jim. In about an hour. See you."

Fletcher had been at the New Era much longer than Jim and furthermore he was a hometown boy.

After ordering a toasted egg and olive sandwich and coffee, Jim asked, "Did you notice the red roses?"

"Yeah. Did you send 'em?"

"Ha Ha."

"Well, you said you were going to ask her for a date."

"I did, but she politely said no."

"They're probably from some guy she knew at the Post. Anyway she's older than you."

"So what. She doesn't look it. Has she gone out with anyone in the office?"

"No. But there's other men around other than the eligibles on the staff of the New Era, for Pete's sake."

Their sandwiches came. They put out their cigarettes and immediately began to eat.

"You don't think my chances are too good, do you?"

"You know that old saying, 'If first you don't succeed'. . . ."

"How old do you think she is?"

"I know how old she is. I'm in personnel—remember. As to any other questions you might have, her resume reads like someone from 'Who's Who' in journalism. There's no skeletons in her closet. She just wanted to work on a small newspaper. She was born down the road in Columbia. She's 5 ft. 7, weighs 121, has curves in all the right places, a face you dream about, and apparently she's already spoken for. "But," as he took another bite of his sandwich, "you have my permission to try again. I don't mind telling you, I'd get in line myself if I didn't have Kathy. She's some looker, huh." He wiped off his mouth and took another sip of coffee.

They lit up again. Fletch reached over and tapped him on the shoulder. "Cheer up buddy. There's other fish in the sea."

"Yeah, sure."

Penny had always loved the water from the time she was a little girl. With her best friend, Daisy Manning, living at Virginia Beach, she tried never to let a summer go by that she didn't manage a visit even just for a few days. And since Sam's cocktail party wasn't until the third Saturday in July, she arranged with the paper to take a few days off. Sometimes she actually got homesick to see Daisy and her family. She would be taking the train out of Lancaster the next night. Her connections were excellent and Daze would meet her in Richmond the next morning. She was packing her jewelry in a little beaded case that her Aunt Mim had given her for Christmas last year. And there it was, her gold heart pin, and of course, this brought memories of his phone call on Tuesday night.

She and Mrs. Donley were chatting on the front porch—it was hot!

"I believe that's my phone," and she went flying in through the screen door.

"Hello."

"Penny. Sam here."

"Hi. It's good to hear your voice."

"Serious?"

"Very. Did you receive my letter with my two big 'Thank-you's'."

"Yes. You're going to have to admit that I am

psychic. I didn't realize the red rose was Lancaster's flower."

"You called to tell me you're psychic?"

"Of course, why else. How's it going?"

"Well, it's hot as Hades here and I'm looking forward to my trip to Virginia Beach and swimming in the Atlantic."

"When do you leave?"

"Thursday night. When do you leave?"

"Early Saturday morning. By the way, do you change trains in Washington?"

"No, and my connection's so good that I probably won't be there more than half an hour."

"Don't make book on it. Do you have your schedule handy?"

"Sure. Hold on."

"Back again—ready."

"I've been ready since April."

"You were born ready. Now listen carefully. If we're thinking to rendezvous in D.C., it'll be brief."

"Short and sweet, babe—I'll take it." She listened. "Well, with your stop at Baltimore add another 45 minutes. I'd say you'll get here at around 11 p.m. Penny even if it were just 10 minutes, I'd take it. All right with you."

"Oh Sam, it sounds great. You really think we can do it."

"Sure. I'll be there and don't worry if you can't get off the train—I'll come on. I have a TV pass. You really liked the roses."

"They were lovely and 'caused quite a stir in the office. Everyone is wondering who my secret lover is."

"I know."

"I do, too."

"Penny I want you to know that Amy thinks you're the cat's meow. She also informed me that you'll make a perfect hostess for the party and she hasn't even met you."

"Sam, she truly is a lovely person and as you said, very efficient. And it appears as though everyone is coming. There is a question concerning Greg and his wife since they'll be on vacation, but I suppose he's talked to you."

"He is coming. So, yes, I believe that's everyone. Thanks again."

"I've enjoyed it. How long will you be gone?"

"Well, that's another reason I called to tell you that my plans changed. I'm not going now until the week after my big bash. The beginning of August was more convenient for all concerned, including my parents."

"But you said . . ."

"I know. Well, I will be getting up early Saturday morning. Hal Conner invited me, rather us—like you and me, to spend the day on his yacht, but, since you can't make it, I'll be going. I'll miss you! However, I may also be swimming in the Atlantic Ocean. Any possibility we could meet there."

"Not hardly," she laughed. "We'd better stick to the railroad station." (Knowing Sam, he wouldn't have too much time to miss her on a cruise ship with pretty little scantily clad beauties trapsing around.)

"Penny?" (She was definitely ticked off.)

"I'm here."

"You got so quiet. I thought for a minute you

hung up on me. I want you to be good on your holiday."

"I will if you will. Good night Sam. (He could feel the wires chill off.)

"Have I got a choice? Now remember Thursday night, I'll find you. Got me?"

"Do I?"

"What do you think? Sweet dreams Penny." (click)

He smiled. She was jealous!

She dropped the heart pin into the beaded case.

CHAPTER VIII

HE KNEW the schedule. It was almost 10:45 p.m. when her train pulled into the station and the stop would be brief. She stayed in her seat, but kept her face glued to the window. Of course, it was raining which didn't help. Then she saw him and he was wet. He must have started at the front of the cars and began working back. He saw her at the same time. Since she was close to the end of the coach, she stood up and hurried toward the exit. God, it was only a month—their visits used to be a year apart. Oblivious to all those around them, they flew into each other's arms. Just hugging, smelling, and touching. That was everything!

His hair was wet and his beard was a little rough, but jiminey, who cared. Close to her ear, he whispered, "Oh babe, I missed you."

"Me too, Tarzan," she answered rubbing her hand through his short, bristly hair.

"Come on," he grabbed her hand, "we can get off for a little while and don't worry I can get you back on before it pulls out."

They got off and stood under the roof which shielded many waiting passengers. In no time at all the voice came through the loud speaker announcing the departure in 15 minutes. They found a little spot almost directly out from her coach. When once again, he pulled her into his arms.

"God this is crazy. I saw you only a month ago, and it seems like forever," the words came tumbling out as he looked into her eyes.

"I know," she said, rubbing his cheeks between her hands.

"You look tired. You're not getting enough sleep. It's those darn hearings."

"You look terrific, and I love it when you sound like a nagging wife."

"Oh Sam, I'm serious. I'll bet you're going back to work tonight."

"No. I just left there and from here I'm going home."

"Promise."

He held up two fingers. "Boy Scout's honor."

"Have you been waiting long?" (She noticed his TV news badge pinned to his shirt.

"Not really. I drank a cup of coffee and then came down here as your train pulled in."

"Oh Penny—just 15 damn minutes." They were hugging again.

"I know."

With his eyes drilled into hers, he said "I did tell you that I liked your freckles."

"Yes. Did I tell you I liked your new haircut?"

"Did you ever! Oh babe, I'm scratching your face."

"Who cares? It feels good to me."

"Lord, you'll be brown as a berry when you get back from Virginia Beach. You've already got such a good tan."

There were moments of silence when they just looked at each other. "Sam have a good time on the yacht."

"I'm looking forward to *our* party."

They heard a last call. "Sam, I'd better get back on."

"I know. C'mon."

They walked over to the coach and waited until some others got on and then he helped her up.

He saw that she was seated, gave her one last quick kiss, and was gone.

He stood outside her window for a minute or two and continued to get even wetter. Then slowly the train pulled out. Damn she was crying. Now wasn't that silly. Since when did Sam Boyer need anyone to cry for him.

As the clickity clack of the wheels brought her closer to her destination, the excitement of seeing Daisy and her family took over. What a wonderful relaxing holiday she would have with her favorite family. She did! Her only regret was how very fast the time flew by. She and Daisy did manage one heart to heart chat before she left, and the next day at breakfast Daisy's one comment to her husband summed up her feelings quite well. "I'll tell you Al if that Romeo lets Penny get away, he'll be the sorriest man alive."

"Well, if you want my opinion, I think he's weakening. Meeting her at the train in Washington, planning his party, and her serving as his hostess."

Daisy crossed her fingers. "Oh Al, I hope you're right."

He called her before he left for Illinois for the visit with his son and his parents in Buffalo. He sounded tired and she knew he was.

Anti-communism feelings were running rampant in Washington. It seemed that wherever you lived in the United States, no matter how minimal the offense, someone was blasting you as Communist and the Washington scene was being televised continually with "hearings."

This had an effect on those who worked in the media and Sam was not exempt. However, his cocktail party was certainly the bright spot during the month. Everything seemed to run smoothly, and if Sam thanked her once, it must have been a dozen times for being such a terrific hostess.

As her mind dwelt on that Saturday, she couldn't help smiling to herself. She had arrived at his apartment quite early and was overwhelmed with the simplicity and yet very tasteful appearance the furnishings reflected. Amy had made certain that it was cleaned for the occasion and it could have been an advertisement for *Better Homes and Gardens*—it was that perfect.

Sam had given her a key a month ago and it was a good thing since when she arrived, he wasn't there. It gave her a few minutes to look around, which she did. She hung her dress bag in the closet of the guest room since that was where she would be changing. Then she looked at his bedroom which was such an improvement from the last time she had seen it. He had snitched a little snapshot from her photo album, which she thought was a ridiculous picture and had it standing on his night stand by the bed. A small double picture frame was centered on the bureau (which she had chosen along with his other bedroom furniture) that contained two pictures of Cal. Sam was right, the boy really did look much like his father. The room was extremely neat and everything in its place for tonight, anyway, she thought. Sam just wasn't all that tidy.

Although she had enjoyed the party and meeting Sam's friends, the highlight of the trip was spending the night with Amy Grantham, Sam's secretary. During one of their many phone conversations, Amy had extended the invitation and Penny had quickly accepted. She liked the older woman and although Sam had implied the Conners had also extended an invitation to stay with them, she'd demurred in favor of Amy.

Amy was an old maid who had taught school during the war, but had decided that she wanted some sort of employment with a little more "pisazz." (as she stated) Consequently, with a degree in business and armed with excellent recommendations she had applied to the most exciting venue in the whole

United States—television. She laughed when she told Penny that there are still some executives who prefer efficiency over a pretty pair of legs. She had proved her mettle and was a pioneer in the television media.

"Believe me," she said, "I have not always been happy with the choice I made nine years ago. Sometimes the stress hardly seemed worth it, that is until Sam Boyer took me on as his secretary. Then I knew being a secretary can be relaxing even with all its demands."

She loved Sam like a son and apparently doted on him more than his own mother ever did. She confided in Penny that his apartment was cleaned by no other than Amy with the help of her niece. She didn't trust just any cleaning woman to do the job. (What a dear person, Penny thought)

Penny occupied one of the twin beds in Amy's large bedroom, and was satisfied to just listen since she was rather tired. She felt guilty the next morning when she knew that she had fallen asleep while Amy was still extolling Sam's virtues, but did remember one last comment. "I knew Sam would have a very fine lady friend, so I wasn't surprised when I learned to know you. For all his blustering and sometimes unsavory words and phrases, he truly is an understanding and considerate gentleman." Penny remembered answering, "I agree," before she gave in to sleep.

She guessed that by now, he and Cal were in Buffalo and even though she knew the trip would be tiring—it was a rest from the rat race in Washington.

"Miss Nagel," her intercom.

"Yes." There's a messenger here with a package for you which you must sign for. All right to send him in."

"Yes."

Penny signed, gave the man a tip and he left.

The postmark was Washington D.C.—she'd just been thinking about Amy and now here she was sending her something.

It was a book. Then she saw the jacket with its impressive picture of a G.I. in the jungle with the title—*38th Parallel: The Korean Conflict,* by Sam Boyer. There was an envelope on top with her name, but not Sam's writing. She opened the envelope and read.

Dear Penny: Sam gave me explicit instructions before he left that should his book come from the publisher while he was gone, it was to be sent to you with his personal note to be placed inside. Amy P.S. The publisher always sends the first copy directly to the author. You have the first copy. Love, Amy

Why did he have to do this? When she opened the book, right inside Amy had placed his note. It was in a plain white envelope with Sam's handwriting—*Penny.* She tore open the envelope and read. (Oh God, tears again) "I gave you my heart, now you're getting my blood and sweat." S.

After she wiped away the tears, she was mad. She didn't want the heart pin, and she didn't want the damn book—she wanted him. However, she did feel quite honored to receive the first book off the press.

When Eva came by a few minutes later to chat, she proudly showed her the first book off the press.

She had just taken the note out and placed it in her handbag.

"Well, according to Sam's secretary, I have received the first copy of his new book."

"Oh Penny, that's what was in the package." She looked at the book and then looked at the back of the jacket where she saw Sam's picture. She looked a little puzzled.

"Oh Penny, he did come in here one Saturday morning with you, didn't he?"

"Yes, I believe you did meet him. However, his hair is different now."

"Of course, I knew something looked different. He sent the roses, too."

"Yes."

Eva never overstepped her bounds regarding boss and secretary relationship, she learned that in high school, but she was thinking plenty.

"You must feel flattered to have received the first copy."

"Well, I suppose I do." She laughed nervously. She didn't want Eva Nolt to read too much into this gesture. Penny knew how gossip could fly around an office and she certainly didn't want that happening. "Sam is unpredictable. He's out of town right now so I suppose that's why I was chosen." (She hoped in her heart that wasn't the reason) After Eva left, she read over her note once again.

A smile crossed her face this time as she remembered his publisher, J.R., and his agent the night of the party. They along with Sam and Hal had formed an impromptu quartet. It was their rendition of *Bill*

Bailey, and their accompanying antics that had everyone in stitches.

Thoughts of the party filtered through her mind when she could see again Sam's reaction to her black and white cocktail dress. Naturally, he waited until the last minute to get dressed, and by the time he made an appearance, she was already in the kitchen discussing some last minute details with the caterer. The man and his wife made a very competent team. She answered the door and took charge of keeping the plates filled and drinks served. Her husband concocted the delicious morsels. They had set up various small tables throughout the apartment, with the exception of the bedrooms, of course, and the most scrumptious hors d'oeuvres were constantly within reach. Penny was just leaving the kitchen after popping a crabmeat ball into her mouth when she bumped into Sam. She knew that he had already sampled a few drinks—claiming to be the official taster. So when he very ceremoniously twirled her around and into his arms, she wasn't too surprised. Nor when after he kissed her, she wasn't too surprised to hear him exclaim that the crabmeat had a great flavor, but when he marched her down the hall toward his bedroom and stopped to fondle every curve he could find and suggested that they indulge in some "special necking before everyone arrives" she decided to call a halt. Even as she answered, the doorbell was ringing. As she wiped the lipstick off his face with a tissue, she said, "C'mon Lover Boy you can't sneak out at your own party."

"You're right, but damn you sure look pretty. Now tell me you didn't buy that dress just for me."

"I can't, because I did."

"Just for me?"

"Yep. You look kind o' cute yourself." She looked lovingly into those big blue eyes. "Now Mr. Host get to that door and knock 'em dead." He did!

The conversation was lively, the drinks disappeared with mysterious ease, as did the food, and Penny mingled.

She discovered one of Sam's bosses was sort of a "kuke," but amongst 18 people—there's bound to be one. The quartet, which drowned out the record player, was urged to continue entertaining. They obliged!

In a brief conversation with Scara, the only female writer invited, she was secretly pleased when the woman said, "So your Sam's best kept secret."

"I hope so."

"You're not what I expected," she said, as she lit another cigarette with the most beautifully manicured hands that Penny had ever seen.

"Oh."

"You've known him for a long time?"

"Ever since college."

"He's a rather complex individual, isn't he?"

"You might say that. Yes."

"Maybe sensitive, but blunt."

"That's good. Yes."

"You're in love with him, aren't you?"

"You might say that. Yes." Penny replied, never changing her tone of voice.

They both laughed.

"However, he was slightly off key in that last song."

"Yeah, you might say that," Scara answered, and they laughed again.

As Penny walked away, Scara had to admit, this woman was exactly the one for Sam Boyer.

Penny never did find out what Scara expected.

A good hostess to the end, Penny was the last to leave, but when Sam insisted on driving her over to Amy's house—she flatly refused. The caterers had cleaned up the apartment and were leaving, as Penny gave him a peck on the cheek and marched him into his bedroom. His tie had been discarded hours ago, so now he began unbuttoning his shirt.

"Your bed is ready and waiting, Sinatra. See you in the morning."

"Yes dear. I love it when you sound like a nagging wife." He was a little unsteady as he began pulling off his trousers.

Yeah sure, she thought. He plopped into bed and was snoring by the time she closed the door of the apartment.

Sam came by the next day and took Penny and Amy out to dinner. Since Amy had politely refused Sam's invitation to attend the Saturday night affair, she was given the honor of choosing the restaurant for their Sunday dinner. She chose the Surf and Turf, and it proved to be an excellent choice.

Penny was very pleased with the arrangements for Sunday. No one but her knew the importance of this outing. That morning she had awakened feeling very depressed with one dandy headache. Her dream was the reason! She slept very little since all night the vision of beautifully manicured hands were around

Sam's neck and he was looking into her dark eyes. Scara had double the amount of sophistication any writer deserved plus an extremely sensual laugh. All of which tended to create a very disturbing dream.

When she called Sam the next morning (which he had requested) to remind him of the time, she would not have been the least surprised if Scaratelli had answered the phone. Instead she heard Sam's sleepy voice, "I'm rising and shining—please, just 10 more minutes." He had just gotten awake.

Amy's assessment of the lead role in her dream didn't help any. She was an excellent writer and well liked by the staff.

She had just finished putting her groceries away after her Friday night trip to the markets in Lancaster. She'd probably gained weight since arriving, but everything always looked so good. As she bit into a fresh peach, however, she was remembering yesterday at this time, which brought to mind that doctor.

She'd gone for a long overdue physical. In fact, she believed the last one she had was about eight years ago. A girl in the office had recommended this guy. Well, she decided that would be the last trip to him even if she choked on a chicken bone. He invented the word "exploratory." He had hands like an octopus—they were everywhere at the same time. (Maybe Grace had gone for a sore throat.) Then when he sent the nurse home and they were there alone, she really became suspicious. After she was dressed and sitting in front of his desk, and his conversation took a definite turn toward personal—she knew there would be no return trip. He was surely married, she thought, and if not, he could get his "jollies" elsewhere rather than with her. She just had a feeling that she'd be hearing from him again, especially when he realized she was a virgin and expressed his surprise with some long medical term. But in the meantime she would do her homework and be ready. Basically he seemed to feel that she was in good shape. (She laughed to herself—wouldn't Sam have a comment for that play on words.) But she was mad, and for two cents she'd do a story on him. Then the phone rang.

"Pen, Sam here."

"Hi. How's it going?" He sounded more relaxed than the last time he'd called right after getting back from his trip.

She'd thanked him for his "blood and sweat." His book was doing very well, and Penny wasn't surprised. It was terrific.

"Surviving. Is this your work-free weekend?"

"Yes, but you already knew that." (She sounded annoyed.)

"God, you're wound tight tonight. A bad scene or what."

"The 'or what' seems to fit. What's up?"

"I'm behaving, so no comment. I can be there tomorrow by ten. Are we on for the weekend?"

Penny hadn't gotten involved with any men. After she'd put Jason down very gently, but firmly. No more! She was concentrating on her work and doing very well. The staff liked her and the feeling was mutual. However, she did have some tentative business plans for tomorrow night. (For some reason tonight she didn't want to be taken for granted.)

"Well," she hesitated, too long.

"Penny, cancel your plans. I need to see you. Please."

"All right. All right." (God, she was really ticked off.)

"Come on. Tell me what's wrong. Remember this is Sam you're talking to and I can tell when you've got a problem."

"Oh it's a combination of things. A little self-pity plus being upset when you called, I'll get over it."

"I want to know Penny, please."

"It concerns a doctor's appointment that I had last night."

Now he was alarmed. "My God, Pen what's wrong?"

She sensed the tenseness in his question, and she was kind of pleased. "There's nothing wrong with me, physically, according to him anyway. Although now I'm not even sure of that. I'll tell you Sam I was rather upset. After last night it'll probably be another eight years before I go back to a doctor again."

"Babe you're talking in circles. Did he make a pass at you?"

"You're getting warm. Let's just say he did much more feeling around than was necessary. Actually he went way beyond the call of duty. Then after he sent nursey home, he came on with the pass. I was so darn mad when I got home that I decided if he sent me a bill, I was going to send it back with a note saying—oh just forget it. I'm cooling off."

"Well, I won't forget it." That sucker got further with her in one night than I have in 14 years just because he's got a frigging M.D. behind his name, he thought, the bastard.

"Now I'm sorry I told you. Don't worry, I can handle him. When he calls, and I'm sure he will—I'll scare him so bad he'll wish he'd never heard of me. I don't work on the number one daily in this city for nothing. You do remember how to find my house, don't you?"

"I can always find you, but for Pete's sake, why you had to be in a row house where they all look alike is beyond me."

"It's what's on the inside that counts."

"I'll keep that thought. You're not going to tell me his name, are you?"

"No. Sam be careful on the drive here tomorrow. That traffic is horrendous on the weekend."

"You worried about me?"

"Always."

"I'll let you go so you can put your groceries away."

"How did you know?"

"You told me about market on Friday."

"You don't forget, do you."

"Not when it concerns you."

"Time to hang up. You're getting smoochy."

"You're right. Sweet dreams Pen."

"Yeah. Bye Sam."

"I'm going up and get dressed. I'm taking you to the hotel that my mom almost bought, until Papa changed her mind."

"That would be The Columbian, right? I'm looking forward to it."

He had loved her story and truly hoped some day that she could share it with the reading public. Penny couldn't possibly imagine how much he wanted to meet her parents since reading their life's story. As she said, they made a beautiful combination.

It was amazing, that even though Penny had so much love for her parents and family, she didn't feel the need to camp in their backyard. She had lived away from home ever since she went off to college, but maintained close ties with those she loved—not stifled by their presence, just comfortable with the knowledge they were there for her. God he loved her and right now he wanted her so bad, he hurt.

He walked up the stairs and heard the shower. He strode over to the bathroom door, and pounded on it. "Penny," he called, "turn the shower off."

"Sam," she yelled. "What is it?"

"Penny," he yelled back, "turn the damn shower off."

Just then the singing and shower stopped.

"Sam why is it you always have to start a conversation when I'm in the shower. Open the door a crack so I can hear you."

"Will you marry me?"

Silence—not a sound.

"Did you hear me?"

"I heard you. Why? Do you want to get me between the sheets."

"Well, yeah, that, too, but there's another reason."

"Let me guess. You want to wash my back."

"Well, we can make it a package deal and include

that, too. But the main reason, if you'll be quiet, is because I'm in love with you."

Silence—not a sound.

"Well."

"Well, what?"

"Will you?"

"Sam, let me think about it while I finish my shower. Okay."

"I'll be downstairs waiting on my answer. Say, I could wash your back while I'm here." (He laughed.)

As he pulled the door shut, something crashed against it—probably the bar of soap.

He went to the kitchen and opened the fridge. Sure enough she had some beer. After taking several gulps, he just stood there with his arm propped against the door.

He thought about that Saturday in July when Hal and Marilyn had fixed him up with a date for dinner and dancing on the yacht. The setting was perfect, and the woman, her name was Wendy, was perfect, too, but he had a lousy time. That was the first time he'd been in their company with a date since Penny (and the blue dress), and Hell, that's all he could think about. He'd been out several times with women since he'd gotten back to the states, but Penny just kept ruining his evenings by not being there. So last night he'd said to himself, this is ridiculous, go for it. All she can say is no, and if that's the case—he'd die old and lonely.

He didn't hear her come down the steps.

"Sam," she said softly from the doorway.

He looked up and there she stood his dirty blond with a little white terry cloth something or other on

and in her bare feet. Her hair was still wet. God! She
looked good enough to eat.

They both went for each other at the same time.
His lips were all over her—eyelids, ears, neck, and
her arms were wound tightly around his neck. There
lips met with their special kiss and Penny could taste
the beer. Gee, it tastes good, she thought. Penny's
arms came down from around his neck and she held
his face between her hands. As their lips parted mo-
mentarily, she looked up into his eyes, and very
calmly said, "Why Sam, why did you wait so long?"

He pulled her to him again, and buried his face at
her throat. He could feel the pulse on her breasts.
"Oh Penny you smell so good and I love you so
much, and I'm an idiot. That's why I waited so long,
I'm stupid."

"I'll marry you, but ask me again, please."

He stepped back and took both her hands in his,
and said with great solemnity, "Penny I love you.
Will you be my wife?"

"Oh yes, Sam, I've loved you for such a long
time."

Then his hands began weaving through her hair,
and he leaned over and whispered, "but I want the
package deal."

She threw her arms around his neck and he swung
her around. Her belt was coming open on her little
beach coat, and he noticed as she did.

"What do you have on under that thing?"

She was pulling it together, nervously, "Not much,
(actually nothing) I was in a hurry to get down here
before you changed your mind."

He was about to burst his zipper, when at the

same time, he caught a quick glimpse of one of her boobs.

Right then he made a decision, painful, but his to make. She looked at him and knew what torment he was experiencing, as she said, "Sam, I'm sorry. I didn't deliberately try to make this difficult for you. If it's any consolation, I want you so bad that I can hardly stand it."

"We've got to simmer down Penny." They pulled apart. "We've waited this long, we can wait a little longer."

"So maybe it's time we get out the photo albums."

"Or maybe I should take a shower, *cold*, or conversation, but please not checkers."

"All right. Conversation is good—with a little necking in between." (Very little, he thought)

"I love you Sam Boyer and do you know if I hadn't met you when I was a freshman, I'd probably be married now with five or six kids."

"Why?"

"You know why, you devil, I was waiting on you to ask me to marry you. But I never dreamed it was going to take you so long. Oh well, my mom was 35 when she had David Marshall."

Once again their lips met. In between kissing, they carried on a limited conversation.

"Let's get married soon."

"I don't believe in long engagements."

"A big wedding?"

"No, but a church wedding."

"Your Papa will marry us."

"He'd love it."

"I brought a ring along."

"You what?" Her voice shot up a few decibals.

"Well, just in case you said yes. (He had a smirk on his face.) I wanted to be prepared." (He continued)

"I can't find the damn thing." He was going through the pockets of his suit coat which was draped over the chair.

"Sam, for Pete's sake, you don't forget where you put an engagement ring."

As he stepped back, he caught her toe with his shoe and she left out a howl.

"Oh God, Penny I'm sorry." He carried her over to the sofa. There were tears in her eyes. It hurt that bad.

He let out a cuss word, "Penny you shouldn't walk around in your bare feet," and he was rubbing her toe.

"I'll be fine. I know you're right. Sam I was just so anxious to get downstairs. I was afraid you'd change your mind or leave. I didn't hear any sound after you closed the bathroom door."

"I did. You threw something at me. Just missed my head."

Sam kissed her toe, "There doesn't that feel better."

"I can't feel a thing. There's a box on the floor at the end of the sofa."

"That's it!"

CHAPTER IX

"Oh Sam, it's gorgeous," she exclaimed as she opened the small black velvet case.

He was on his knees rubbing her toe and she was admiring her ring, when the door bell rang. Then the phone rang, "Sam would you get the door and I'll get the phone."

She hobbled over to the phone.

"Hello Penny."

"Papa, how good to hear your voice."

"Honey, I tried to get you last night but your line was busy. I wanted to tell you that we would be in Lancaster today for a meeting and would stop by for a few minutes if it was all right. I wasn't able to get you this morning and I just now got out of the meeting. Is this a bad time?"

"Of course not. Is Mom with you?"

"Yes. She's been in and out of the stores and markets all day." (He didn't tell Penny that they had driven by her place earlier and noticed the Washington D.C. car.)

"Where are you? Gee Papa please come over right now. Okay?"

"See you in a few minutes." (They were just a couple of blocks away.)

"Penny, that was some kid selling candy for his band trip," he said, as he put his wallet away and handed her a huge candy bar. He glanced at her toe and wondered if she should soak it in some kind of water.

"It's going to be fine. Feels better already since you kissed it. That was sweet of you to buy the candy."

"Sam my lip is beginning to hurt, now." His lips came down on hers.

"Does that feel better?"

"Oh yes, you have no idea what healing powers you have. We're getting company."

"We are!"

"Papa and Mom."

"Now?"

"In about two minutes."

Now he was flustered. "Oh God, what will they think?"

"They'll think you're wonderful. Just be yourself—well almost yourself."

"What does that mean?" He grimaced.

"Well you might watch those nasty 'one-liners'."

"You're not going to put some clothes on?"

"Good Lord, you're getting awfully prissy suddenly. I'm 34 years old and we're engaged."

"But Penny, he's a preacher."

"Sam, you did read my manuscript, didn't you?"
He nodded.

"Okay. Relax. Let your coat where it is. My parents are coming. They won't like you any better with your coat on."

Penny did button the little terry-cloth beach jacket (it came *almost* to her knees) and pulled the belt in tightly, before opening the door.

After hugging and kissing, Penny looked toward Sam and then toward her parents, and said, "Rebecca and Pen Nagel, Sam Boyer, my fiancee." Penny couldn't help being amused at Sam's apparent embarrassment. She never thought she'd see the day.

They all decided on a little white wine which Sam offered to serve, but Penny wouldn't hear of it and left for the kitchen.

She was listening to the conversation as she fixed the tray with the goblets of wine.

Congratulations in order . . . Yes, just five minutes ago . . . she's limping . . . I stepped on her toe . . . I read your book . . . terrific account of the conflict . . . knew each other in college . . . we know.

"Here we are. Did Sam tell you we just became engaged less than ten minutes ago?" She sat on the sofa beside her mom after serving each his wine.

"Yes, and I think this occasion calls for a toast, don't you Rebecca?"

She was lovely, but Sam should have expected as much. After reading the book, he knew she was very young when Penny was born. They could almost pass for sisters. And the preacher—he just didn't fit

Sam's profile for a man of the cloth. There was such love apparent between the two, and Sam didn't know that existed at their age. He was amazed!

"Indeed I do."

They all rose and the Reverend Pen Nagel said, "To a wonderful daughter who I am sure will make a terrific wife, and a loving mother, and to Sam whom I am certain can afford to buy her shoes. We wish you both a long happy married life filled with love." He and Rebecca laughed as their eyes met.

The ice was broken with the crack about the shoes and they all enjoyed a special camaraderie as they drained their goblets.

"Mom do you know where Sam and I are going to dinner tonight—The Columbian. Would you and Papa come with us and help us celebrate. If that's all right with you Sam?"

"Only if you wear that outfit. It sort of grows on you."

Penny's father spoke up, "Oh, I don't know Sam. I think a beach umbrella might add embellishment."

"Mom isn't my ring just lovely," and she held her hand up under the light in the ladies room at the The Columbian, "and it fits."

"Yes, dear it is, and the young lady wearing it is lovely, too."

"Spoken like a true Mother. You like him?"

"I've always liked him."

"But Mom, you just met him."

"Not really. I've been hearing about him for years."

Oh yes, Rebecca and Pen knew Sam Boyer, the man who won their daughter's love. His appearance,

however, wasn't exactly what Rebecca had imagined.
His and Penny's coloring—eyes, hair, and skin-tone
were almost exactly identical. They could have been
brother and sister. He wasn't quite as tall as Rebecca
expected. She guessed he was about 5' 11"—in fact,
just about the same height as her husband. She had
drawn a mental picture of the incomprehensible
Sam and had actually expected a Cary Grant. He
looked so suave on the book jacket, but in person
with the short hair—he looked like a regular G.I. Joe.

On the personality, she could take an A+. Although he was tough on the outside, after spending
the evening with the two of them, he was just a big
marshmellow on the inside. And Rebecca knew that
he could talk his way "out of a paper bag" and that
smile! Penny was right. It could melt an ice cube in
January—maybe even a whole tray.

Penny hugged her mother. "Oh Mom, I know
what you felt that day at the Lake when Papa asked
you to marry him—again."

Rebecca knew that her daughter was in love for
the very first time in her life. It had taken awhile, but
true love is worth the wait. It was for her. Secretly,
Rebecca was glad that Sam Boyer had come to his
senses, finally.

"I know Penny. It happens only once. In some re-
spects, he reminds me of your father. You know
something else. You're both almost the same ages as
Pen and I were when we finally married." (Penny had
already drawn that parallel.)

"Mom you haven't asked me, but I'll tell you why
I wasn't dressed when you came."

"That's not necessary."

"I know, but I want to tell you. Would you believe that I was taking a shower when Sam proposed. I went upstairs to get dressed for our dinner date, and I heard a knock on the bathroom door—well, more like a clap of thunder. So I turned off the shower, and he says, 'Will you marry me Penny?' God he's such a jackass. I told him that I'd give him an answer when I finished my shower. Naturally, I already knew what my answer would be, but I wanted to hurry downstairs to tell him before he changed his mind. Well, that little beach robe was the first thing I grabbed. According to him the ring was an after thought in case I said yes."

Her mother laughed. "Well as I said, he reminds me of your father. Remember me telling you before we went to Maryland, I had time to buy only tooth-brushes." (Penny remembered all right, it was in her book.)

They would be married the Saturday after Thanks-giving. Penny did hear from that doctor again, and she told him to take a flying leap, the lecher. The Lancaster New Era received Penny's two-week notice after only six months.

Daisy was called to serve as her matron-of-honor. Barney Edwards would serve as Sam's best man. Penny would meet the Boyer family and Sam would meet the Nagel clan. Penny would have one month to send invitations to friends and relatives and buy a wedding gown. She would contact her old friend, Roberta, to sing. And of course, all the while Papa and Mom would become enamored by Sam's magnetic personality and realize very quickly why their only daughter was so much in love.

"Barn I'm nervous—nervous as Hell. I never thought that I'd get myself in this marriage bit again."

"C'mon Sam, I hope you're not comparing this with the way you screwed up the last time. Remember I was there for that one, too. You're getting a real woman this time around. In fact, I can't believe she waited on you all these years."

"Well, you could say that I've waited on her, too."

"Oh, that's right you never did score with this one."

"Nope."

"Damn, I'd like to be a 'fly on the wall' tomorrow night."

The two had just gotten back to their hotel room. They had reservations for three days prior to Sam's wedding on Saturday. Tonight they'd completed the run-through for the wedding, sort of a rehearsal, and Barney was sure impressed with Penny. Secretly, he felt that she was probably worth the wait. He knew his old buddy well enough to realize that this marriage would last. He envied Sam!

"Don't rush me Barn. It's not tomorrow night, it's Saturday."

"Yeah, that's right. Tomorrow night we men get our chance to 'rub your nose in it'."

Sam was pulling off his socks. "You really like her, Barn."

"She's a doll. Consider yourself lucky, buddy. To my way of thinking, there's just no comparison between her and that other one."

"You know Barney I've thought of that other experience many times during the past eight years, and
I've decided that I just jumped the gun. She was
beautiful, she was the first (after getting back to the
states), and her family was so impressive. I never
loved her. I know that now."

"It took you eight years to figure that out. I figured that out eight months after you were married.
You may not remember but you did mention Penny's
name to me many times during those early years. I
can still remember the letters that she wrote and
how much they meant to you. In fact, if the truth be
known, I sort of thought she was the *one* way back
then."

Sam had just gotten into bed and had his hands
folded under his head lying on his back. "Barney,
you're probably right and I was too stupid to face the
truth. She was always there for me. She was my an-
chor. Hell, I guess you could even say she was my
inspiration. You know what she said to me the night
I asked her to marry me. She said, 'Sam, why did you
wait so long'? For some hot shot writer, I sure was
one dumb bastard."

"Okay, we got that settled. You have plenty of
good years left and knowing you, you'll take advantage of every one. So why the jitters?"

"Oh Hell, I'm not sure! Regardless what anyone
says this is an important step, and I sure don't want
to disappoint her. I don't want to be a two-time loser
and screw up again."

"You won't—no way. You two are so much in love
that even in that crowd tonight, you two were alone.
I noticed."

"Okay Barney, I'm convinced. Now how about your marriage. There's still hope, right?"

"Sure. We're getting things ironed out. It takes time. We'll make it buddy."

After dousing their cigarettes, Barney looked into the darkness and thought, God he's so blessed. I hope Fran and I can find what he has with Penny Nagel.

Sam didn't go right off to sleep either. He was remembering Barney's comment "being a fly on the wall," but where. He still felt apprehensive regarding their motel accommodations.

Two weeks ago he and Penny had spent about an hour in consultation with Pastor Nagel which was his general practice before marrying couples—even if half of the couple happened to be his daughter. Sam continued to be amazed by his future father-in-law. The man had an uncanny insight into the minds of his fellow human beings, almost to the point of making one feel uncomfortable about his past. However, all his suggestions for happiness centered around one word, love. God's love and love for each other. (Sam kept remembering Penny's book.)

They were driving back to Lancaster, when he told Penny that he planned to make reservations at a five-star hotel on their wedding night.

"No."

"What does that mean?"

"Sam I don't want an elegant, grand and glorious room on our wedding night."

"Why not?"

"You read my book. You do remember the kind of place where my parents spent their first night?"

"Sure I remember—The Cozy Inn Tourist Cabins."

"The faded drapes and bedspread."

"Yes, I remember."

"Well, there aren't many tourist cabins around anymore, but there are small no-name motels."

"You want some flea bag motel because your parents started out a step below the ritz?"

"Sam, please humor me on this. We only have a day or two anyway. I promise next summer when we really have our honeymoon, you can treat me to CLASS."

He looked at her. She was actually very serious. "You're nutty, you know that."

"You having second thoughts?"

Sam laughed and pulled her over closer to him.

"Babe, I could make love to you in a barrel. You go ahead and set up our reservation, and lead me to it."

But once again, he began to wonder. Damn! I hope it has a bathroom.

Penny was married on the Saturday after Thanksgiving in 1954, and Papa married her and Sam in Trinity Lutheran Church.

The Reverend Pen Nagel married his first-born, and only daughter. Secretly, he and Rebecca were wondering if Penny would ever find her true love. They were convinced she had. This was a profound experience for the minister and one he would never forget. Penny was a creation of God that bound he and Rebecca together over many, many years.

He had faith that his daughter and Sam would find the same happiness granted to him.

They had a gala celebration afterward which included a delicious meal, dancing, and the convergence of two families—the Nagels and the Boyers. Sam's "laid-back" parents and his family were overwhelmed with the informality, love, and closeness of the Nagel clan, and would never feel quite so relaxed and blessed again. They were immediately drawn to the effervescence and inner beauty of their son's wife, and knew this time he had made the right choice.

The experienced globe trotter, author, and journalist who had served in two wars was marrying a small town girl who had captured his heart many years ago and refused to let him go.

Penny's parents understood all too well. The same thing had happened to them many years before.

It was after five, when Penny and Sam quietly left the party. They would be spending the first night in a motel outside of Philadelphia, which would be the beginning of a brief honeymoon since Sam had only a few days. Their real honeymoon would come next summer.

"Min, this is Bill."

"What's wrong?" When she got a phone call, it scared her.

"My truck broke down outside of Philly, and I'm stuck at a motel tonight. I'll probably be pulling out in the morning. Min?"

"Yes, what is it." (He didn't sound right.)

"Well, I won't get much sleep tonight. The

damnedest thing happened. The room next door has a pair of honeymooners and they've been humping and going at it ever since they checked in about two hours ago. "These walls," and he chose several cuss words to further describe how thin they were, "aint good for much. And that damn bed sounds as though it's coming right through. I tell you Min my head's throbbing."

Min began laughing. "Sounds entertaining to me. I'll bet you're about to bust a gasket."

"It aint funny Min. My gasket already busted once and may again, if Sam—that's his name, doesn't soon give it a rest. If his little lady says 'Oh Sam' one more time, I'll have to sit in a cold tub."

"What's her name?"

"What the Hell does it matter? I think it's Patty. Men don't call out names when they're busy pumping."

"Oh Bill, (she tried to sound sexy), when will you get home."

"Not soon enough. Hold on a second. It's gotten quiet. Damn! Now they're taking a shower and I believe she's singing. God Almighty, what next."

"Bill, how do you know they're newlyweds?"

"I can spot 'em a mile away—saw 'em when they checked in. See if you can get your mother to keep the kids tomorrow night."

"I'm going to call her right now. Hurry home."

"Goodnight Min."

"Goodnight Bill. Sweet dreams."

"Damn!"

Bill glanced down at the tatoo he had on his arm. When he left the Navy after the war, he was so

proud of Min right in the middle of a heart inter-
twined with roses. He decided to check with the ter-
minal again regarding his truck.

He knew for sure that would be the last time he'd
stop at the Suburban Motel.

(Bill might have been more understanding had he
been privy to the following conversation.)

They had just left the gas station where Sam had
paid the boy extra to wash off the "just married"
from the back of his car while he took down the
notes pinned to the inside.

That damn Barney had certainly been busy. It was
his own fault, really. When he mentioned locking
the car, Barney had laughed and said, "At your age,
and already married before, who in the hell could
embarrass you." Sam knew—now! Barney could and
did. God, one of the notes was pretty raw. That was
the only one he didn't show Penny. It was taped to
the steering wheel. In fact, they wasted at least a half
hour at the damn gas station. Finally they were on
their way.

It was dark and Sam glanced over at Penny and
asked if she wanted to turn on the radio.

"No. Sam, I was just thinking, I hope I won't disappoint you tonight."

"What makes you think that?"

"Well, you know. After all you've been married
before and had experiences with other women, and
me, well I've never . . ."

"I know Penny. You're a virgin, aren't you?"

"Yes, and I don't know. Oh you know what I mean."

"I'm not worried. You're a fast learner."

"But if I'm . . ."

"Then we'll practice. We'll do it over and over and over again."

"Oh Sam, you're so understanding—I think."

"You nervous?"

"Well yes, maybe a little."

Silence.

"Babe I love you, and I'll be very patient," he said, as he reached over and felt for her hand. "You're certainly not the first virgin on her wedding night, and I'm sure you won't be the last."

"I did set up an appointment with my aunt as you suggested, and she was very helpful. She let me know, too, that Sam Boyer was worth the wait. Thought I'd pass that bit of news on to you."

"Penny, she is such a lovely person it's difficult for me to comprehend that she is actually a doctor. She and her husband make a striking pair. Now let's see, she's related through marriage—she and your dad were really cousins. Then later she became his stepsister. Right?"

"You're learning. It'll take a while, but I'm expecting you'll have a long time to study the genealogy chart."

"Oh Babe, I really hope that I never let you down."

"I hope you do."

Sam laughed. "Wow! What have I created? My wife has developed her own one-lines."

Penny was giggling, but stopped long enough to

say, "I just couldn't resist. Believe me, it will never happen again."

"Are we nearing our destination?"

"Yes."

"I hope so," he growled. "What's in that white box in the back seat."

"That's my pretty white lacey gown."

"Oh."

"What are you wearing?"

"Me. What am I wearing?" He laughed. "Nothing. I hate over-dressed teachers."

"I have a confession to make, but promise you won't laugh."

"Okay."

"I never saw a naked man before."

"And you had three brothers."

"I said **man**. They were little boys when I left home."

After a period of silence, Penny said, "Sam remember that time when you opened the door and you were standing there in your shorts."

He hesitated, then, "Yeah. Yeah I remember—you were mad at me."

"Well, I wasn't really mad at you. I was upset with myself."

"Why?"

"The sudden appearance of you almost naked really set my hormones off, and I just could hardly stand to look at you."

"You're serious?"

"Yes."

"Geez, I didn't know I was so sexy, and even in my old shorts." He whistled.

"No laughing, please."

"Damn Penny, I don't understand. I know, your brothers were little. How about men in bathing trunks?"

"They were just two and seven when I left, and swim trunks are different from undershorts. I never saw a naked man."

"Well Babe, you will tonight. In fact, all night." he added.

Silence.

"I just thought I'd tell you that I was fitted for a diaphragm."

"Well, I hope you didn't get it from that gigalo in Lancaster."

"No, of course not. Aunt Mim took care of that detail."

"Good. I'm glad."

"Sam, you're not really a perfectionist, are you?"

"I am tonight."

"Did you talk to my aunt?"

"No. Why?"

"She figured you for a perfectionist—**tonight.**"

"Geez, I just love Aunt Mim. I wonder if she'd be our family doctor."

"Sam that's our motel up ahead on the right side."

"At last. It's about time."

After Mr. & Mrs. Sam Boyer were signed in, he locked their door and pulled their drapes closed. The room wasn't too bad.

That night her life was fulfilled and she was truly blessed with the love of Sam Boyer. Damn, that nightgown had cost her "an arm and a leg," and she didn't even get to wear it.

According to Bill, and we only have his word, Penny and Sam worked hard for perfection on their wedding night, and upon hearing them in the shower, we must assume that Sam got the package deal.

They went on that delayed honeymoon seven months later in the summer, and Penny did have the opportunity to wear her expensive gown; however, by this time she was pregnant.

They vacationed in Hilton Head in supreme luxury and they both decided that it wasn't a bit better than the Suburban Motel. With the love Penny and Sam shared, they did not need the added incentive of a chaise longue.

CHAPTER X

EXACTLY ONE year after Sam and Penny were married they had a son. And, at Penny's insistence, he was named Samuel Carson Boyer, Jr.

"God, Penny how will you be able to stand two males with that name. (Sometimes he wondered how she put up with him.)

"There's a Penny and Pen in your family and now there will be a Sam and Sammy in ours."

"Just watch me, Big Sam," she laughed, as they discussed the name in the hospital.

"Where did this Big Sam come from anyway. I'm not that big."

"Oh, I don't know, I think you're pretty big."

"Do you really, babe?"

"Well, I really am not able to make any valid comparisons, but you're about all I can handle."

He stooped over and kissed her, as he whispered,

"And I want you to know that I'm ready to be handled—in fact, I'm overdue."

"That makes two of us."

He noticed her full breasts with the nipples pointing straight out, her shining blue eyes, and her tangled hair and decided that she was the sexiest new mother that he had ever seen.

"Babe how long before we can have sex?"

"I already asked Aunt Mim and she's going to give us a booklet with all the information regarding the how, where, when, and why."

"Well, the when and where might help, but we don't need any info on why or how."

"Sam remember when we first married and I told you that I had much to learn."

"Sure, I remember. I also told you that you were a fast learner, and I was right." (Geez, was I ever, he thought.)

"Sammy is proof of that. You were a great teacher."

He kissed her again. "Gee, Penny, you're embarrassing me."

"Oh Lord, that'll be the day."

"Penny, did you notice Sammy's dinger. I think he's going to take after me."

"God forbid." She covered her eyes and laughed. "Oh, that hurts my stitches."

"Stitches? Penny I didn't know you had stitches. Where? Why?"

"My opening wasn't large enough for Sammy, *and* his dinger." Then she couldn't help herself; she had to laugh again.

Then they both laughed. "Well, it's your fault—making fun of our little boy."

This conversation brought to mind some really stupid, ass-hole remark Connie had made when Cal was born.

"Oh Sam, I love our little son, but when the time comes that we can't laugh—God help us. You're pensive. What are you thinking about?"

"Nothing important, believe me. You're right and Babe I think that I love you even more now than we were married if that's possible."

"Sam move my red roses over here closer so I can see them first thing in the morning when I wake up."

He did and he gave her that dazzling smile, "You really like my roses."

"Bullseye."

Just then the door flew open and in came the nurse carrying Sammy. They could both hear the sucking noises he made with his mouth and smiled.

"Geez, he's hungry Penny."

"That's okay, I'm loaded."

"Visiting hours are over Mr. Boyer."

"Just a few more minutes, please."

"All right, but only for you." (She was a sucker for that smile of his)

"You're a doll, Smitty."

Sam watched as his son found Penny's nipple and began his lunch. It was the first time he'd witnessed this marvelous fete and he was overwhelmed. (Connie had refused to nurse Cal and Sam hadn't questioned why.)

"Does that hurt?"

"No," she said as her hand gently brushed the top of Sammy's bald head.

"God, that must taste good. He's sure putting it away." He stooped over and kissed his son on the cheek that was puffing in and out. "He sort of looks like me, doesn't he Penny."

"*Sort of* is putting it mildly. If he has any Nagel at all—I haven't seen it yet."

"Cheer up, Babe. The next one will."

"Is that a promise?"

"Yep. That comes in lesson number 21. Now I must get out of here before Smitty kicks my butt."

"Bye Sam. Hang in there until I get home."

"It isn't easy, but I'll try." He stooped over and kissed her, and then he just couldn't resist and moved his lips down and kissed her boob. "See you tonight," and he was gone. (He'd left his two boxes of cigars, but it was too late to call him back.)

Smitty was waiting outside the door looking very impatient in her starched uniform.

"Checking on me. You didn't trust me; now tell the truth?"

"I was just checking to make sure your watch wasn't running slow."

"God, you're tough, but I love you," and he reached over and kissed her on the cheek.

Where were guys like Sam Boyer 20 years ago when Marietta Smith was looking for a husband, she thought.

She could still smell that woodsy scent mixed in with her palmolive soap. What a man!

Penny was more sure every day that she wasn't wrong in waiting. She looked forward to a wonderful life with Sam and their family, and once again she silently thanked God.

When action started in Viet Nam, Penny knew Sam had the itch to go. She would not try to influence his decision. Their family had grown to five, and they both knew that was final. She had a difficult time with Becky two years later, and the doctor came close to recommending that she have a hysterectomy. Of course, when Phil was born 16 months later—the doctor was certain it was time to tie her tubes. They all agreed!

"Oh, they'll have a good time. I didn't know they'd be so stubborn—not wanting to attend a college reunion."

Rebecca's husband looked at her and said, "We'll have a good time, too, you know, taking care of our three grandchildren. So let's get to it!"

Rebecca looked at her husband, the Reverend Pen Nagel, and said, "Let's make a deal. I'll look after the baby and you take charge of Sammy and Becky."

Reverend Nagel held the hand of the little girl who looked so much like her grandmother. He couldn't classify her as cute. She had a little too much pepper and not quite enough sugar and spice, but she was *charming*. She allowed herself 100 per cent advantage from every attribute which she possessed. Consequently, in that department, she rated an A+.

Now Sammy had so much of his father and didn't really take full advantage, so that there were times the Reverend had to *get tough*. He and Sammy had quite a few serious talks during the visit, so that by the time his parents returned, Grandpa and Grandson had a splendid relationship. The Reverend had raised twin sons who were an institution within themselves, so he knew just *one* Sammy was no reason to panic. However, two Sammys, he decided, would have been an unwelcome challenge.

Rebecca dearly loved this little fellow, not only because he was named after her own true love, but he was just so cuddly and sweet natured. Phil had all the good qualities of both parents, plus a few extra from God. In fact, he was so well behaved, it was frightening. She'd heard Penny and Sam mention several times what a pleasant little guy he was. So naturally, she was very pleased with the *deal* she'd struck with her husband. Although she loved all three, Sammy and Becky needed a stronger hand, and Pen met that requirement.

Rebecca was so concerned for her daughter when she realized that she was pregnant for the third time. She and Pen had spent a great deal of time praying. It was touch and go for awhile, and Sam came very close to insisting that she abort. The doctor would surely have agreed. Penny was stubborn and promised everyone that this would be the last. Actually, the doctor came very close to advising, that after Becky, it would be prudent to tie her tubes. Well, the Lord rewarded them with a treasure when Phillip was born. And of course, Penny knew she was right in insisting. She and her husband, however, both agreed before she left the hospital that their family was now complete.

Rebecca checked on Phil once again before climbing into bed. He had a little skunk that he dragged around everywhere and he was holding it next to him. He was already sound asleep. Her children had all kinds of stuffed animals when they were little, but a *skunk!* No one needed to tell Rebecca where that came from. That surely was Sam's idea.

Rebecca and Pen were so pleased when Penny and Sam were married. They were a match even though they were very different. The secret to the *match* was love. They were so very much in love with each other and certainly old enough to realize what marriage involved.

As Rebecca reached toward the night table for her glasses, her eyes fell on the picture of Sam, Penny, and Sammy when he was a year old. She'd never forget how Sam made a trip to Philadelphia to just hand out cigars when his son was born. In fact, she remembered that he had visited just about all the relatives. (It was difficult to imagine that he had fathered another son. He truly loved children) He really was quite a Dad.

Oh he was different all right! One had to look beneath the surface to catch his *daddy feelings,* but they were there, always.

She laughed to herself when she thought of the incident that occurred during her Easter visit.

Sammy and his little friend, James, were playing after school on the swing set and Rebecca was sitting there reading, watching, and listening which can be very educational when eavesdropping on two second graders' conversation.

She heard James ask Sammy why his dad didn't go to PTA.

"He can't."

"Why? Does he have to work?"

"No. That's not the reason. The reason is my mama won't let him."

James had stopped his swing and Rebecca had stopped reading.

"Why won't your mama let him. My mom lets my daddy go."

"Oh-h," Sammy hesitated. "Cross your heart and hope to die—kiss a dead snake if you tell a lie. Promise you won't tell."

Very seriously James promised.

(Rebecca did, too.)

"Daddy says it's because Miss Gates is young and pretty, and Mama's afraid he'll like her too much."

Just then Becky came out to the swings and the conversation ended.

Yep, he was different, all right!

Penny was so good regarding the children's religious education. The one she had the most trouble with was Sam. He went to church, but one couldn't consider him a steady customer. Most of the time Penny gave him an *E* for effort. It was understood by all that if his father-in-law were the minister, he'd go every Sunday. So Penny held that thought, until . . . She was privy to a conversation between Sammy and Becky on a recent Sunday morning.

Sammy said, "Daddy's not going to church this morning."

"How do you know?"

"Cause I'm a boy and Daddy told me. Girls don't know."

"Maybe I already know," she said rather flippantly.

"No way, but I'll tell you if you promise not to tell anyone."

"Can't I even tell Mama?"

"No way. You can't tell Mama."

"Oh all right," she said, reluctantly.

"Well Daddy said if I hear him breathing heavy on Sunday morning that means he hasn't slept well. You know like congest-tian when you get a cold. This happens *to men*, and I just cracked the bedroom door and listened, and he's breathing heavy. So I know he won't be going."

Yep, he was different, all right!

Was it just this morning that she heard herself saying, "It's a deal."

Rebecca held Phil and Pen grabbed on to the other two. They closed the door after waving "good-bye," and their task began.

However, their thoughts were on another new war, of sorts, beginning on the other side of the world. They both knew Sam's penchant for wanting to be where the action was during a war. They both had secretly hoped and prayed that there would never be another challenge to face their son-in-law. If Sam felt the need to be over there with the troops in this latest crisis facing the United States, they both knew their daughter would not stand in his way. Penny understood and loved her husband and if he felt the need to go once again to a war front, then he must follow his conscience!

Knowing their daughter so well was the main reason the elder Nagels had been so insistent that Penny and Sam take this holiday and attend Penny's college class reunion. Neither said so aloud, but both felt this could possibly be the last reunion for Penny and Sam.

This would be a most important event. They would be returning to the scene of their first meeting and the beginning of their love which took so long to reach maturity. Yes, this was very important for many reasons. So important, in fact, that a few hectic days with three little ones to watch over, (when they were both in their sixties) was no sacrifice at all. However, they laughed at the thought, there was a distinct possibility of their domain in eastern Pennsylvania being declared a war zone.

The last words Rebecca heard before falling asleep, completely exhausted, were Sammy's, "Grandpa tell me once again how you hopped on that freight train when you ran away."

Wonderful, wonderful children, she thought, and how rewarding to be grandparents.

"Geez Sam, I really feel guilty leaving the kids with Mom and Papa."

"Come on Babe. You know they'll have a "ball" and plenty of help, too, I'm sure."

"Just hope Becky's diarrhea clears up."

"She was fine this morning. You know she gets that way every time we're going on a trip."

He looked over at Penny, whom he was sure was ageless. She just kept getting more attractive after each baby. Of course, he knew that there would be no more, and he'd just have to settle for that forty-something beauty sitting beside him. The dirty

blond hair was getting lighter, with a little grey pene-
trating; the blue, blue eyes still sparkled; and her
body still drove him wild. No one would ever guess
that she had born him three children. He was lucky
as hell! Now if that ruckus hadn't begun in Viet Nam
—life would be perfect.

"Sam, you're right. Let's look at this as sort of a
third honeymoon, okay?"

"Say, I'm ready. I'm always ready for honeymoon
celebrations. You did make the reservation at Boer's
Head?"

"Oh yes. Daze and Al will be right next door."

"God, I hope they're not adjoining rooms. They're
a nice couple, but when I wrestle with my wife, I
don't want anyone around." (Sam would be Sam until the day he died.)

"Bullseye. I may even wear my nightshirt. The
rooms are 121 and 123."

"You're all heart, you know that. I was hoping tonight you'd be in the buff." He reached over and ran
his hand up her leg.

"I will if you will."

"It's a deal." He laughed.

"Penny get your hand away from there, I'm driving."

"You could have fooled me. Keep your hand out
from under my dress."

She should have expected as much. After all he
had been gone two weeks on an assignment and had
just gotten home late last evening. Then Penny was
up and down most of the night with Becky.

"All right. All right," he grumbled. "How many

miles to Charlottesville. I bet we're not even half way yet. What did that last sign say?"

"No."

"The sign said "no?"

"No. You're right. We're not half way yet. Sam do you want me to drive?"

"Why would I want you to drive? After all, you hardly slept last night. You need your rest."

Geez, she thought, was he ever touchy. "Well, you do sound rather impatient and out-of-sorts."

"Just because I'm getting a little **feel**. You used to like that."

"Oh Sam, I still do, but not when you're driving on a two-lane country road." She straightened her dress, and said, "Think of the fun we'll have seeing people we haven't seen for 20 years."

"My mind just refuses to hone in on old class-mates."

"Ha! Ha! Once you take a gander at those pretty little numbers you used to date, you'll probably let me in the hatcheck room."

"Don't fret. I'll pick you up before I leave."

"I might get picked up sooner, Lover Boy."

"You wouldn't dare, and you're asking for it."

"Guilty as charged."

"You're going to get it, too."

"I'm counting on that."

(Their dialogue was once again back to normal.)

The class reunion was fun, and they really did enjoy seeing their old friends after all these years. Rock and roll had replaced the Bunnie Hop, and Elvis Presley had replaced Frank Sinatra, but most of their classmates did their own thing on the dance floor which included Penny and Sam.

Daze related to Penny some of the comments she picked up while mingling. Most were quite surprised that Penny had married Sam Boyer, but there were a few who weren't. In fact, Amanda Shannon's statement came to mind. "I sort of had a feeling that those two would end up together. You know for all his 'playboy' antics in college that I remember, there seemed to be something special he had for Penny Nagel." Oh yes, Daze knew. She had always known.

Penny had picked up a few "vibes" herself. She had some small talk with Dan Fletcher. He seemed surprised that she had married Sam Boyer.

Penny and Dan had dated several times when she was a senior. Never serious. He had a girl waiting back home.

When she'd asked him *why*, his only comment was—Boyer didn't seem your type.

He's not, she thought. That's why I love him so much.

"Goodnight Daze and Al."

"How about coming in for a drink you two?"

"Okay with you Babe?"

"We don't have a curfew."

The four had arrived at their rooms after all the goodbyes, hand shaking, and kisses had ended.

The men busied themselves preparing the drinks after shedding their coats, loosening their ties, and turning up their shirt sleeves.

The women shed their shoes and propped their feet on the bed.

After discussions on who had gained weight and who had remained most attractive, and naturally the husbands and wives, they all agreed it was a fun evening, and planned to come back in 1981.

"I think I'd better take my date home—she's falling asleep."

"It's the wine."

"I married a lush."

"You weren't supposed to tell."

"Damn. I forgot."

He came over and put on her shoes, as he said, "C'mon Babe, Papa will tuck you in."

As they headed toward the door, Daisy reminded Penny that she was owed a letter. "Sam bring the family to Virginia Beach next summer."

"You're crazy! There's five of us."

"I know."

"Can you supply a life guard for each kid?"

Penny spoke up. "Could I have one, too?"

"One what?"

"Life guard."

"Oh, I've got one lined up for you."

Penny put her arms around his waist and rested her head on his chest. "Does he have hair here?" She poked his chest.

"Goodnight you guys and thanks for the drinks." He kissed her on the top of her head. "Penny you're embarrassing me." He laughed. They all laughed.

As they walked out the door, they heard Penny say, "That'll be the day."

When Penny came out from the bathroom, Sam was sitting in the dark waiting on her. She could hardly keep a straight face. She had on one of her old night shirts.

"Good Lord, what have you got on?"

"My night shirt."

He put out his cigarette and walked over to her.

"Turn around."

"The whole way around?"

"Sure."

Very carefully, and rather gracefully, she thought, she did as he asked.

"Which is the front?"

"Sam Boyer, you're insulting, you know that."

"I bet I know," he said, laughing, as his hands went up under the night shirt and found her boobs.

They were ready for their honeymoon celebration.

Of course, Sam and Penny had their peaks and valleys—all marriages do, but nothing earth shattering, and their love only grew stronger.

Sam's hair got a little thinner and he wore his specs more often. Penny's figure wasn't quite the perfect measurement it had been, and her dirty blond kept getting lighter, but they still made a striking couple wherever they went.

Their kids weren't perfect either! Sammy was big-time, and never took the blame for anything. Becky was Daddy's little darling, and since she looked like Penny, couldn't do anything wrong. Then Phil, being the baby, was revered by all, especially by his name-sake, Reverend Phillip Eugene Nagel (Pen).

But they were, by and large, a close-knit family who attended church regularly—even Sam. (Well, he went most of the time)

Sam still felt his wife had the sexiest little ass on

this side of the Potomac, and Penny knew her husband's smile could still melt an icecube in January. So when he decided to go to Nam, he went carrying the love of his wife and family, and the best wishes of all. (Penny called him the Bob Hope of correspondents.) He just couldn't let a war happen without being there, but she prayed and prayed that this would be the last. She just wanted him to come back! Before he left, his third book was published, entitled, *Inside Washington: The Hearings.*"

CHAPTER XI

SHE laid Sam's letter down after reading about the crude shower the guys had constructed and remembered some poignant history from a year before. As always, she was in the bathroom when Sam wanted her attention. (She smiled to herself.)

He proposed to her in the bathroom. She saw him naked for the first time in the bathroom. She believed her first-born was conceived in the bathroom. Now she was in the bathroom again and he was tapping on the door. They had just made wonderful love and she had slipped out of bed thinking he was asleep, to take care of some personal hygiene.

"Babe may I come in?"

"Sure." She had just wrapped her damp body in her big towel. (God him and his bathroom visits. Here we go again.)

He stood there in his shorts, wide awake, and just matter-of-factly stated, "I need to go to Nam."

His eyes never left hers, but he didn't move.

Why wasn't she surprised. President Kennedy had been assassinated the year before, and President Johnson was now sending men there in record numbers. She just knew it would only be a matter of time before Sam would get the urge to go.

She walked the short distance between them and his arms came out and pulled her to him.

"Penny I won't go if you just say the word. I'd be leaving you with three small kids and a hell of a lot of problems, but I had to tell you what I feel in my gut. Can you understand?"

They kissed, sweet, loving kisses, and she saw the torment in his eyes.

"Oh Babe, I love you so much, but I've been fighting this battle within myself for weeks now, and I just had to let you know."

"I know," she said softly. "I know everything about you Sam Boyer, and if I didn't love you so much, I couldn't let you go." (God, she thought, I hope this is the last war in our lifetime.)

She glanced out the window at her kids playing in the yard. Sam had been a good provider. They lived on their 2.5 acre farm in suburban Alexandria and had just finished the pool before Sam left for Viet Nam.

As she watched Becky splashing her brother, she thought of the time Becky had contracted the measles. Penny had called Sam at his office with the doctor's diagnosis. Consequently, the minute he walked in the door he hurried up to her room. He stooped over and kissed her on the forehead. "I understand that you may be in bed for awhile. Mama says that the measles got to you. Is that right?" He sat down beside her bed.

Her little face puckered up, very close to tears, as she said, "Daddy maybe you shouldn't visit me. Have you had the measles?"

"I don't know. Is that important? My dad was in the military and they didn't bother too much with measles."

The tears started dropping as she held her arms out to him.

He took her in his arms and after taking care of her tears with his handkerchief, he said, "Now you listen to me Becky honey. I have only two girlfriends, you and mama, and I'm not leaving here. Right now you need me more than Mama."

"Do I get three wishes?"

"You sure do, but you know the first two don't count."

"I know Daddy."

"All right," he said, as he felt her head. She had a little fever.

"I wish you would tell me a story while I'm eating the chocolate ice cream you brought."

"You're a little con artist, you know that, but I can't resist. I'll be right back."

After she had finished her ice cream and he had finished his story, which held her spellbound (as always), he said, "Now that your wishes have been fulfilled, I think you'd better get some rest."

She crooked her little finger beckoning him down

to her. He stooped over and she hugged him with both arms as she said, "I love you daddy."

"Oh Becky honey, I love you, too. Goodnight and sweet dreams."

"Daddy, does Mama know I'm your other girl-friend?"

"She sure does, and it's okay. Say your prayers and I'll stop by in the morning before I go to work."

That night Penny checked on her before going to bed, Becky looked up and said, "Mama, I love my daddy."

"I know honey. Mama does, too."

It was rough when the kids first found out that their dad was leaving. They didn't understand. She and Sam sat down with them and explained why he had to go, and at times the situation was practically insurmountable for Penny.

They had met in Hawaii once since his departure —that was almost seven months ago. It seemed more like seven years.

When she checked into her hotel, she found that Sam had already registered. The attendant accompanied her to the room along with her luggage. Upon opening the door, she spied the florist box on the bed. She knew! There was a dozen beautiful, beautiful red roses. The card nestled between the green tissue read—I love you. S.

As tears rolled down her cheeks, she became cognizant of the shower blasting away. She brushed the tears from her eyes and laughed. Naturally, she should have known, the bathroom.

She quickly undressed and put on the new peignoir that she had bought for the occasion, and walked into the bathroom. She tapped on the glass. Slowly, the glass panel moved to one side and she glimpsed a soapy, wet Sam. Their eyes met and held, as she said, "Hi Sam. Is there space in there for me?"

"Oh Babe, is there ever."

The peignoir slipped to the floor as he helped her into the shower. She looked into those hungry blue eyes glistening with water-tipped lashes, and said simply, "I've missed you Sam."

His arms went out and he pulled her into his soapy wet chest as he whispered in her ear, "Same here Babe."

After the longest shower on record, they emerged to sprawl out on the bed and talk and talk, and look and look, and touch some more. His hand moved over her flat stomach.

"No more babies."

"No, you sorry?"

"Of course not. I'm thankful you had Phil without complications. God Penny, I was so scared. I came very close to telling the Doc to end the pregnancy. First and foremost, I wanted my wife." (Penny knew the trying time that he had been through. She had thanked the Lord many times. Especially since she had been so insistent on having the baby.)

They swam together, walked together, and played together.

They toured the islands, Pearl Harbor, learned the hula, and ate pineapples. They even rode horseback one day. Even though Penny was not an accomplished equestrienne, she did know enough to stay in the saddle. Sam was quite good. In fact, before Viet

Nam interfered, he had toyed with the idea of buying the kids a horse.

The most treasured moments were those spent in
conversation regarding the children, his and her families, showing him the many snapshots she had
taken, and listening to the kids' tapes. He had questions and she supplied the answers.

He was mesmerized by her walk, her voice, and
her looks. He knew this week would have to last him
a long time, and damn he almost felt as though he
and Penny were meeting each other for the first
time, and God it was great!

They went to a play, to a movie, and one night
they danced on the roof garden. He requested **The
Nearness of You** and geez they played it.

Penny remembered his whispering in her ear,
"What's this do to you?"

"I'll never tell."

He pressed his lips to that part of her neck right
under her ear. Sam continued to be her lover and
God she loved it.

When they arrived back at the hotel that night
there was a bottle of champagne compliments of the
Nam guys.

"Damn, why did they have to go and do this."

She couldn't help notice his eyes glistened with
tears. He pulled out his handkerchief and blew his
nose and wiped his eyes.

He had made it plain there was to be no references
made to the war. Penny realized the gift of champagne would be the closest Viet Nam would come to
entering their visit.

And then the four days were over. She boarded the

plane for the states and he waved goodbye going the
other direction. And yes, it seemed like seven years
ago.

Penny returned to reality and Sam returned to un-
reality.

He sent tapes for the whole family to hear, and
these were wonderful. It seemed as though he were
right there in the same room with them. This form
of communication was certainly an improvement
over letters. (although they continued to exchange
letters, also)

Like how do you tell him on a tape that Bonkers
died.

The kids had found the little dog in the field
shortly after they had moved into their home. He
was a little puppy of questionable origin, skinny and
boney, but with a tail that wagged. They all immediately fell in love with him and christened him
Bonkers Boyer. Oh yes, he was so much a part of the
family that he even had their last name.

This practice, of taking dogs and cats out into the
country and just leaving them, wasn't unusual, but it
was a cruel practice by persons who wished to rid
themselves of unwanted animals. The kids went
"bonkers" over him the first day, and he was added
to their menagerie which included a cat, two ducks,
and a rabbit.

There wasn't another dog in the whole world like
Bonkers. He loved the outdoors and running free. He
had never had a collar or a leash on him. It didn't
matter what that dog was doing or where he was if
one of the kids or Penny called, he came and right

away. When Sam left, it was with the knowledge that Bonkers was there with his family and he was assured of a built-in security system.

The dog had grown to the size of a German shepherd. He had a mean set of teeth and an aggressive bark, which caused any apparent foe to take heed.

And then one day, they found him dead in the field next to their house. They never knew what happened. Together the four of them buried him and put up a wooden cross.

They cried for a week. Penny missed Sam! It was times such as this when her heart ached and she needed that male shoulder to lean on.

The story of losing Bonkers went into a letter, a long letter.

They acquired another dog later on. Their grandparents, the Boyers, gave them a collie for Christmas. They called him Trigger after Roy Rogers' horse. Trigger also proved to be a good watch dog, but he needed more coddling. And, of course, he was no Bonkers Boyer. No dog would ever mean as much to their children again as that first emaciated, little puppy.

Oh yes, this is when Penny missed Sam!

What upset Penny the most concerning the war was the fact that many people didn't even seem to care about the guys who were over there. At first she stayed on her "soap box" constantly, but as time went on, she gave up. She resolved not to go into any detail and when someone wanted to know where her husband was—she would very calmly say, "He's in Viet Nam." She talked to the children and they agreed that Daddy's war service as a correspondent made him pretty special, and on all their tapes to him, this point was emphasized over and over. Sam always received 100 per cent support from his family. Penny knew that made his job less stressful to perform. Sam had not been drafted—he'd volunteered. There was a difference!

It was true. There were times when she needed Sam desperately. The kids were a great comfort. Her parents, relatives, and friends were terrific. And, of course, her faith in God was an ever constant prop when her spirits sagged. But she wanted Sam!

Sam was making a name for himself. His accounts of the lowly G.I.'s (the ones who couldn't evade the draft and the kids who were unwilling to try) and their exploits of heroism and sacrifice were his subjects in every aspect of this horrendous war.

He was her Sam, and she was so proud of him. She prayed every night that the Lord would bring him back to her and his family.

Several years later, Sam did get back from Nam, but not in one piece. He had been wounded in his left arm, and although he kept the arm—it was practically useless.

"Oh Babe, it feels so good to hold you in my arms again—well, in my arm."

Penny held him tightly, never wanting to let him go. He was her Sam, and she loved him so much it hurt.

"Sam, I cannot let you go again. Please don't ask me."

"Penny, sweet Penny, the next time I go," and they clung together, "it will be an act of God."

It was at this point, Phil reached for Sam's limp

arm and caught hold of his sagging hand. He rubbed the hand against his cheek, and as he kissed it, he looked up and said, "Daddy everyone will be using your other hand, so I'll just keep this one for me." He just stared down at the little boy, and then . . .

For the first time in their married life, Sam cried.

He had witnessed such horror, such heinous acts, and God so much death, that he wondered if he could ever again be a responsible father or a **man** for the woman he loved.

It took two months but it happened. He was sitting at his desk trying to write. Penny had come up quietly behind him and reached over his shoulder turning off the desk lamp. Slowly, he turned around. She had moved back into the shadows. When she noticed his eyes focused her way, she slowly stepped into the slash of moonlight that cut across the rug. She was naked!

He put out his cigarette. He stood up and stared. He let out a gasp as though sucking for air, and then almost in a state of shock, she heard that rich baritone voice reach out from the darkness, "Oh Jesus."

That night they both came alive again for the first time since he returned. Sam knew he had served in his last war.

Penny's precious moments of their reunion that night would live with her forever.

It was a year or so later when Sam had a phone call from his son, Cal. He had enlisted in the Air Force. After spending two years in college, he had decided to enlist in hopes of selecting the branch of his choice. He wanted to be a pilot.

Penny had just gotten in the door from a meeting.

"I just hung up from talking to Cal." Sam was sitting next to the phone in his study.

"Oh, I'm sorry I missed him," she said as she planted a kiss on Sam's forehead.

"Come on Babe. You can do better than that."

He pulled her toward his lap.

"Sam I'm getting too heavy for lap sitting." She laughed, as he tugged her down with his good arm.

"Let me be the judge," he answered, as he kissed her.

Sam was Sam again, she thought, as she landed on his lap.

"This is Sam, the judge. You're right Babe. Let's sit on the sofa." They both laughed as they walked over to the loveseat and sat down together.

"Cal's in the Air Force and headed for Viet Nam."

"Oh Sam." She searched his eyes for signs of reaction, but there was none. He kept a blank stare.

"Do you want to tell me about it?"

He did. In great detail he told her everything concerning his son's enlistment and final destination. He summarized by saying, "The last time I spoke to him right after returning to the states, he sounded very much like he intended to enlist. What could I say? It's hell over there, and I don't want you coming back in a body bag. He's the grandson of two career soldiers, and *my* son. All I could say was 'you'll make a hellava pilot, and they're sure needed over there.' Let's just hope and pray that they'll all be coming home before long. Johnson's not running again and if Nixon's elected, he says that those boys *are coming home*, and he'd better deliver. The damn war's going no place. They can't win! Maybe by the time Cal graduates and is awarded his wings, the powers-that-be will see the futility of sending these kids over there to lose a war."

As he lit another cigarette, he looked at her and said, "I'm proud of him, Penny. Hell, he even calls me Dad now."

Penny knew he was putting up a brave front, and she couldn't let him see her concern.

"Do you know where he'll be stationed?"

"Probably Langley. He said he's coming east."

"He'll come to see us, I know. That's so close. And if not, we can go to see him."

"Oh, he'll come after his training is completed. He's a Boyer! They always do what's expected." He looked at her and winked as he found her hand and clasped it in his.

"I know a Boyer who even does more than what's expected—he loves deeply and puts others before himself. Even if he won't let me sit on his lap any-more."

"Oh Babe," his voice was husky, "you really think he loves me."

"I know he loves you."

"Let's try that lap thing again."

Just then Phil came into the room in his pajamas. "Mom I'm hungry. I can't get to sleep."

Penny looked at Sam, and said, "Tact. That was never a strong point with the Boyers."

They laughed.

Gradually their life regained some normalcy. Sam

had much to be thankful for since he was right handed, and was heard to make the comment that God was looking out for him. If everyone knew of the horror and misery he had witnessed, they would have understood that one useless arm was a small sacrifice. That would be the last war Sam would cover and when his book came out several years later, *Viet Nam: The Gutless Wonders*, that would be his last book. Well, possibly . . .

"Hey JR wait up."

Sammy waited until Josh caught up to him.

"Hey man. I hear your old man is going to be the commencement speaker."

"Yeah, how about that."

It was in between classes at Jefferson High, and as it turned out several kids came by and high five'd Sammy. They had also heard that Sam Boyer, war correspondent and author of the best seller *Viet Nam: The Gutless Wonders*, was to be the graduation speaker.

"How long have you known?"

"Not long." He hurried into his next class.

Sammy hoped the old man wouldn't embarrass him. His dad was a writer, one of the best, but geez a speaker.

After the introduction, his dad went to the microphone. He always held a pencil in his left hand. (His was a Bob Dole type of injury) He walked straight, with no hesitation in his step, and very calmly recognized all the VIP's.

Then he fairly yelled into the microphone,

"BONZAI," and threw up his right fist—like he was leading a charge into battle.

Then he waited, and just looked out at the audience. Finally when it was utterly still, he continued.

"I want everyone to remember that because it is a battle cry, and I hope to God you never hear it again. Because that means war and war is hell, and that's not why God put you here." His words rang loud and clear.

Gosh, Sammy was amazed. He had no idea the old man could be so forceful. He glanced around covertly, and realized all eyes were on the podium. Geez, he was proud!

Sammy remembered the last part of the speech, too. In between he was just too excited.

"I've kicked around this globe at various intervals during my lifetime, and I **know** that there is no better place on the face of this earth than right here. No country is perfect, and that includes the United States. We'll always need prisons and we'll always need policemen, but on a scale of one to ten, I challenge you to find any country that supersedes ours.

Respect this land, cherish this land, and thank God every day it's yours."

Sammy looked over to where his mom was sitting, and she was crying. He knew they were tears of love.

There was another person in the audience that day and he also needed his handkerchief to wipe moist eyes. He was a captain in the U. S. Air Force. Penny had written and asked him to try and come to hear his father deliver his first public speech. Capt. Calvin C. Boyer knew that would not be the last speech his father would be called on to make.

That night there was quite a graduation party in the Boyer home. Penny had provided a "Nagel-kind-of-reunion" that Sam had *never* experienced. His sisters, their husbands, his nieces and nephews, Cal and his wife, his grandchildren, and his three treasures, Sammy, Becky, and Phil.

Sam had never in his life felt quite so honored and humbled at the same time.

Barney, his old war buddy, stood off to the side and observed. Sammy was the honored guest, and Sam did his best to direct all attention toward his son. However, many would not be deterred and extolled their praises on the commencement speaker. Barney chuckled to himself. He'd never seen his buddy quite so frustrated. Served him right! God, he was terrific. Of course, Barney was convinced that Penny had much to do with writing that speech, and even now as he watched his old buddy, he realized Sam's eyes were roving all around. He was searching! He was searching the crowd for one person, and Barney knew the minute he had located her. Sam very discreetly slipped away toward the dining room where Penny was standing. He took the tray of petits fours from her hand, placed it on the table, and they disappeared from his view. Sam had found the one he sought. This kind of love had eluded Barney. This kind of love eludes many people, he thought.

What a shame, too!

EPILOGUE

PENNY FINALLY had her book published under the title *My Sister, My Spouse.**

Upon reading the treasured manuscript, her mother through tears of joy, exclaimed "Your father would have been so proud of you."

Rebecca was amazed by the data and accuracy of the facts accumulated by Penny Nagel Boyer in writing the life story of her parents.

Rebecca remembered the Song of Solomon and how often she repeated those words during her married life, and now Penny had taken the words from that book of the Bible as the title of her book. What a wonderful daughter!

Mrs. Rebecca Nagel died eight months later at the age of 82. The Reverend Pen Nagel preceded her in death by nine years.

---

* This is another of the author's books.